OVER EASY

THE CONTINENTAL BREAKFAST CLUB - BOOK ONE

PAMELA FORD

AINE PRESS

BOOKS BY PAMELA FORD

THE CONTINENTAL BREAKFAST CLUB SERIES

Over Easy

Fresh Brewed

Honey Glazed

THE BACHELOR NEXT DOOR SERIES

Love on the Lane

Dancing on the Drive

Breathless on the Boulevard

Romance on the Road

Kissing on the Corner

STANDALONE NOVELS

To Ride a White Horse

Over Easy - Revised Edition
Publishing History
Aine Press digital revised edition published February 2017
Aine Press digital edition published May 2016

Cover design by Robbi Strandemo

❀ Created with Vellum

To all the silly friends who brought laughter to my life: Amy, Carolyn, Cathy, Dinah, Ellie, Liz, Nancy, Patti, Sally, Sue, and Terri.

ONE

Something really needed to change.

Unfortunately, as it was turning out, that something was my life.

I came to this unsettling conclusion one night when Megan, Bree, and I were lifting weights at Better Fit, the fitness club in Minneapolis where we had signed up for free, one-month trial memberships. Not because we wanted muscles (although they were a nice bonus), but because we wanted to meet men.

In theory, it was a great idea—there were lots of guys in the gym. But in reality, after twelve consecutive days of pumping iron after work, our plan had yet to deliver. Lots of muscles, yes. Interested men, not so much. All of the guys seemed to care way more about how many pounds they could power lift with their bulging, tattooed biceps —*guns,* they called them—than the three, *attractive* women in form-flattering spandex doing curls two feet away.

"Allie, this is not working," Bree puffed out from the bench press that night, arms trembling as she pushed the barbell up.

"Maybe you should use smaller weights." I reached for the bar to give her a hand.

"Not the exercise. The men." She was lifting so much weight—for her anyway—I was surprised she had enough oxygen left in her brain to think about anything other than preventing herself from getting crushed beneath that barbell. Then again, Bree had been fixated on finding a guy ever since her boyfriend dumped her, so maybe the thought was simply a reflex action. Like blinking when you go out into the sun. Or jerking your leg when the doctor taps your knee with a rubber hammer.

Bree lowered the bar to its holder, then sat up and eyed a sweaty, overbuilt guy grunting as he leg-pressed what appeared to be three thousand pounds. *Grunting.* Believe me when I say this, guys, grunting is not a turn-on. If you can't move the weight without making noise, cut the poundage. We really, really don't enjoy picturing you creating a hernia. Or worse.

Bree shoved her short brown hair behind her ears, grabbed her towel, and strode across the fitness center toward the juice bar, all the while muttering under her breath. Megan and I exchanged a look and dropped into step behind her, happily leaving the weight machines, cross-trainers, exercise bikes, treadmills—and their panting inhabitants—behind.

Clearly it was time to regroup. And not a moment too soon, as far as I was concerned. I was running out of time. I needed to find a guy impressive enough to bring to my parents' forty-fifth wedding anniversary celebration next month. Not because it was a milestone anniversary, but because my whole family would be in attendance, and having a "keeper" on my arm would be the perfect way to show all of them that, yes, I had reached adulthood.

This whole idea came to me a few months ago, after my parents didn't tell me that my grandmother was in the hospital—dying—until she had been discharged, alive and well. I only found out when my mom called and said, "Allie, honey, good news. Grandma made it."

"Made it where?" I asked.

"She didn't die."

"Was that a possibility?"

"Oh, honey, we didn't want to worry you, but she's been in the hospital since last week—her lung again. The doctor didn't think she'd make it. Father Joe even gave her the last rites."

For God's sake, I'm nearly twenty-eight. I'm enlightened and liberated (yeah, I understand that looking for a boyfriend kind of contradicts that), support myself (sure, Grandpa shoves a twenty-dollar bill in my hand every time he sees me but that's not my fault), live on my own (okay, with a roommate), pay my bills (mostly on time), am informed about world affairs (more Twitter than CNN.-com, but I'm working on it), and even run my own business (although I really need to get more customers—and I'm working on that, too).

And, yet, my parents and siblings still treat me like *the baby*.

I never get told the bad news until it's past. My dad can't stop himself from reminding me to floss. And it goes without saying that I sit at the kids' table for Thanksgiving dinner.

It doesn't help that I come from a long line of over-achievers. My oldest brother is a surgeon, my sister and other brother are lawyers, just like my parents—for once, could they try to be original?—and me, baby of the family, was supposed to be a veterinarian because I love animals. Except after graduating from college, I couldn't bear the thought of studying another day, let alone four more years. So I moved into a lower flat with Bree and started a pet grooming business, *Flawless Paws*.

Now I groom dogs. Big ones, little ones, hairy ones, bald ones, smelly ones... My parents are mortified. "Allie Parker, *doggg groooomer*," is the way my mother says it, her voice sinking progressively lower with each syllable. Not that she has anything personally against dog groomers; it's a fine profession—for someone other than her daughter, that is.

Anyway, I was complaining about this to Megan and Bree when we were watching The Bachelorette and critiquing the prospective fiancés. "My family treats me like the baby," I groused during a commercial.

"But you *are* the baby," Megan said in her best *this-defendant-is-guilty* voice, because, yes, she's an attorney. And though she isn't nearly as know-it-all as my own family members who are lawyers, she does tend to think she knows best, which would be a bit irritating if she wasn't usually right.

"Hard to get around that when your nearest sibling is fourteen years older," Bree said.

"And married," Megan added.

That's when it hit me. The solution was so obvious, I couldn't believe I hadn't thought of it before. If there was anything that would make my family begin to respect me as an adult, it was stepping into that oh-so-grown-up institution, marriage. I shoved a fistful of popcorn in my mouth as I mentally searched for flaws in my thinking—and found none.

"What I need is a husband," I said.

"Hear, hear," Bree chimed in. "But I'll settle for a man."

This, of course, led to a discussion about where to find single men, which in turn led us to Better Fit and free, one-month memberships. It had seemed like such a perfect solution. The fitness center was full of men—and that was just what I needed.

So there we were, striding across the workout room like a team of race walkers in the national championship, about to embark on my favorite part of belonging to a fitness club—the juice bar. After we settled into tall chairs at the bar, Megan and Bree both ordered something new, a cucumber cooler, while I went for my usual chocolate milk, the perfect recovery drink.

The guy behind the counter was wearing a T-shirt made out of one of those moisture-wicking tech materials, the fitness center's slogan emblazoned across the front: *Better Fit makes everything Fit Better.* I couldn't argue with that; his biceps were bulging out of the arm openings and the shirt was so tight I could see the outlines of his sculpted six-pack abs.

"Time for Plan B." Bree picked up her glass. "Nearly two weeks and not one nibble among the three of us. Clearly, we aren't going to find men here. *And I need a man.*" Bree may be a self-assured, beloved high school math teacher, but she sure doesn't do *single* well.

I had to agree. "If I'm going to have a potential life partner to impress the family at the anniversary party I can't afford too many more days buffing up."

Megan shook her head, her curly dark hair bouncing. "Maybe we should give it a rest. Husbands are so...ugh."

She had married at twenty-one, divorced at twenty-two, and wanted nothing more to do with the institution. But then, she was an attorney not a dog groomer, so try as she might there was no way she could totally relate to my concerns about being treated like a baby. Not that there's anything wrong with dog grooming. I'm just saying.

"You know how your arms feel stressed and shaky

when you've lifted a really heavy weight too many times?" Megan said. "That's what marriage is like."

"Too young," Bree said.

"Wrong guy," I added.

"Are you with us or against us?" Bree gave Megan a pointed look, then took a big swallow of cucumber cooler and grimaced as it went down.

I'm never sure what's in the different drinks the juice bar sells—generally carrots and lemon and radishes and stuff—which explains why I stick to chocolate milk after exercising. Bree eyed my glass. I tightened my grip on it and gave her the stink eye. She'd made her choice; she needed to stick with it.

Megan heaved a sigh. "Online dating?" she said without conviction.

"Church groups?" I offered.

Bree snorted. "Who do either of you know that online dating or church groups has worked for?"

I opened my mouth.

"And don't tell me about Joey Neander because he really, really is the only person *ever* who met someone at a church social."

And Joey, as my Irish grandmother used to say, had a wee bit o' problem with the drink. So a teetotaling Baptist girlfriend was exactly what he deserved. "How about a young professionals group?" I asked.

"Gag," Megan said.

"Coffee shop?" Bree proposed.

"Oh, please." Megan took a big swallow of juice. Based on her expression, I didn't think she liked the cucumber cooler any better than Bree did.

"If you aren't part of the solution, you're part of the problem," Bree said.

"How could I possibly be part of the problem?" Megan asked. "It's not my fault there aren't any single guys left."

"Okay, Ms. Negative Force Be with You." Bree held up her index finger. "I challenge you to come up with an idea, just one, for how we can meet single men ages twenty-six to thirty-five."

"That's the only criteria? Twenty-six to thirty-five?"

"Intelligent," I interjected. "Not necessarily rocket scientists, but smart enough."

"Fun, but not party animals. And reasonably attractive," Bree added.

"With decent jobs. After all, these are our future husbands, we don't want bottom dwellers."

Megan ticked off the list on her fingers and asked, "Anything else?" as though once we had nailed down the requirements she'd be able to deliver the goods.

I rubbed the bridge of my nose, thinking. What sort of man would make my parents—*I mean, me*—happy? "I've narrowed it down," I said. "What I want is an S man. Single, straight, sober, solvent, stable, successful."

"And slung," Bree added.

"That's hung," I said.

"Whatever. He just better bring it."

Megan almost choked on her juice, then nodded thoughtfully.

Bree and I exchanged a grin. This was great. Once Megan put her mind to something, the rest of the world better get the hell out of her way. I took a chug of my chocolate milk and waited, confident that a solution was only moments away. But as the moments stretched into minutes, I began to despair. Could it be that even one of the world's preeminent problem-solvers was stumped by this one?

Then Megan gave a Mona Lisa smile, small but so full of promise you knew she had an awesome idea, one so good it might just make you burst. She pressed her hands onto the counter and leaned forward. "When I was in college and broke—"

She stopped so abruptly, I knew she was having second thoughts about sharing what she'd been about to say.

"Yes?" I urged her.

"I'm not proud of this."

"We've all done things in our youth that we regret." Bree waved an impatient hand. "Come on, spill it."

Megan blew out a breath between clenched teeth. "Okay. I used to put on nice clothes and sneak into continental breakfast at hotels."

"You mean like, donuts?" I asked.

"Donuts, bagels, cream cheese, waffles—"

"We're trying to get married," Bree said. "Not fat."

Megan ignored her. "At almost every table would be

some guy, alone, dressed to kill, fueling up for a morning business meeting."

The meaning of her words hit me with such force I jerked upright on my stool. "And?" I asked, almost faint with the possibilities. Adrenalin surged through me and I felt renewed. How many hotels were there? How many continental breakfasts? How many men, glorious men, were at breakfast waiting to meet the women of their dreams over blueberry waffles and raisin bran?

"And, unlike the guys hanging out in hotel bars, the men at continental breakfast wear their wedding rings." Megan grinned at us, then finished off her juice and triumphantly plopped her empty glass on the table. "Instant, irrefutable identification of marital status."

Her words delivered the luscious fulfillment of a morning bun on an empty stomach.

"Omigod," Bree said on an exhale. "You are so worth every penny of that six-figure income they pay you."

"Did you ever get caught?" I asked.

Megan shook her head. "Look like you belong, act like you belong—"

"And you belong," Bree said breathlessly. "But how—"

"Side door. Just fumble in your purse like you can't find your key. And when someone leaves—"

"You're in." I couldn't believe the brilliance. "At the very least, we'll get a free breakfast."

"And at the very best, we'll meet eligible men," Bree said happily.

Megan tapped her fingers on the countertop. "As your attorney I feel compelled to warn you—be careful what you wish for, you might just get it."

"One can only hope." Bree laughed and gave her head a shake.

"Amen," I added. "Here's to finding the men of our dreams."

By the time we left the gym, we had the beginnings of a plan. Bree would do some reconnaissance at a couple of nice hotels to get the lay of the land, the scoop on each continental breakfast, the location of the side doors, and anything else we needed to know to look like we belonged. Once she reported back, we would set a date and time for our first foray. And then—I almost shivered in anticipation —The Continental Breakfast Club would commence its first breakfast meeting.

I couldn't stop grinning as I drove home. This could be the best manhunting idea anyone had ever come up with. Ever. In the history of the world. And so simple. Like Megan said, just put on nice clothes and—

Nice clothes? That would mean like skirts and jackets and heels...or something. My enthusiasm dipped. These would be professional men, maybe even executives. They would expect to see their peers at breakfast, dressed for big sales presentations, corporate takeovers, company buyouts. A nervous tremor slid through me. Nice clothes for me meant jeans without dog hair and soapsuds all over them. And somehow, I was pretty sure that showing up in jeans at an upscale hotel's continental breakfast wasn't going to convince anyone I was a professional on a business trip.

I made a desperate face at myself in the rearview mirror, as though Reflection Allie might miraculously deliver a solution.

Bree probably wouldn't have any trouble figuring out what to wear—after all, she was a high school teacher and had to dress up for parent/teacher conferences and open houses and sometimes even on school days. But whenever I needed to look nice for an event, I lifted something from my sister's closet. Jen may be fourteen years older, but we're exactly the same size. Okay, fine, she's a little smaller, but if I hold in my stomach, I can totally wear her clothes. Anyway, she has impeccable taste. And, as a lawyer married to a lawyer—yes, she married a man of the same ilk—Jen has the money to indulge her every designer whim. Which means, I can indulge my every designer whim just by borrowing clothes from her.

And holding in my stomach.

Problem was, if I called Jen and asked to borrow business clothes, her mental antenna would instantly be up and rotating, her legal mind whirling, calculating, deducing. And if she mentioned it to her husband, Peter, well, let's just say that, between the two of them, I'd be tried and convicted before I even said a word.

I pulled to a stop at a red light, grateful to the Department of Transportation for providing me a moment to mull over my options. I knew I couldn't borrow anything from Bree—she was the ultimate petite size and I...wasn't. Not only was I four inches taller, but my weight was a sliding scale—ten pounds up, ten pounds down, ten pounds up. And, I currently wasn't on the leaner side of life, so the fitness center membership had been a nice plus.

My point is, I wouldn't have fit in Bree's clothes on a good day and certainly not that week. As for Megan's clothes, maybe, but highly questionable because she is, well, much curvier.

Which meant that my only choice was to borrow from my sister. Which also meant I had to be prepared to navigate the deposition she would surely put me through when I arrived looking for business attire. Obviously, the element of surprise would be helpful. I needed to show up unannounced, preferably when both Jen and Peter were busy. I glanced at the dashboard clock. Eight-thirty. I was almost guaranteed that they both would be totally engaged in getting their kids to bed—a five-year old girl and twin three-year old boys. I could picture the routine that was playing out at that moment—baths, snacks, books, tantrums, drinks of water...repeat at random. With any luck, I could grab some clothes and be out of there before either of them even thought about switching into high interrogation mode.

Channeling my inner stock car driver, I whipped through a U-turn when the light changed, and aimed my silver Civic onto the freeway entrance that would shoot me in the direction of my sister's home. I had fifteen minutes to come up with a plausible explanation for why I needed to borrow some clothes, a reason so close to the truth I could say it without sounding like I was lying, a solid rationale that Jen wouldn't even consider challenging.

In my mind, I stepped into her oversized walk-in closet and slipped my feet into a striking pair of black heels trimmed in black patent leather. Suddenly, my legs were longer, more shapely, my posture divine, my brown hair streaked with gold. I tossed my head and my hair slipped silkily across the back of my neck. *"Well, you see,"* I would say coyly as I slid a hand over a sleek charcoal dress on a hanger. *"I've, ah, met a man."* I would let that thought sink in just a moment before following with, *"He's quite successful...in real estate development. So many properties, you know, are available now that the economy has bounced back. It's really a buyer's market."* Then I'd smile and go in for the kill. *"And, promise me you won't tell Mom and Dad, but I'm meeting with the dean of the vet school next week."*

I couldn't hold back my grin. Genius, pure genius. That combination of incentives had to be enough to get me an armful of Jen's very finest designer duds, no questions asked.

My plan worked perfectly. I headed home with three professional outfits hanging from the hook above my car's back window, and only a teense of remorse over my explanation for needing them. The only reason I had any guilt at all was because my sister had gotten way more excited about the vet school than she had about the man. And the vet school bit was, sigh, truly a bold-faced stretch of the truth, whereas there really was a man involved—I just hadn't met him yet.

But, oh, let me tell you, the clothes were fabulous.

TWO

EARLY THURSDAY MORNING ONE WEEK LATER, WE CONVENED the first Continental Breakfast Club meeting at the Tucker Point Hotel, a fine upscale establishment frequented by successful, out-of-town businesspeople. Though all three of us would be in attendance, only Bree and I were actually going to breakfast. Much as we tried to change Megan's mind, she resolutely refused to join us, insisting that she would set up shop in the first floor ladies lounge to be our support team, our pit crew if you will, should Bree or I need advice or help along the way. To be honest, I don't think she wanted to be there at all, but she felt guilty that she'd given us the idea and wanted to make sure we didn't get in any trouble.

We drove to the hotel separately so we could all go to our jobs afterward. As the clock ticked closer to our six-thirty a.m. rendezvous, Megan put us on a three-way call to run through any last-minute questions. She pulled along-side my car at a stoplight and gave a wave. "Allie, are you still planning to go in first?" she said into her phone.

My stomach flopped and I gave a quick nod. "I just don't want to get caught. It would be humiliating."

"Don't worry. The staff will be so busy with check-outs and keeping the buffet filled, no one will even notice you."

"Why would anyone ask? In Nan's clothes you look so professional." Bree's voice blasted out of my Bluetooth headset. Obviously she had us on speakerphone and was shouting to make sure we heard her. "When I'm in my forties with two kids, I hope I look as good as she does."

"Yeah, well, it helps that she has a lawyer's income," I muttered. "And she got our Mom's genetics. Unfortunately, I inherited my Dad's."

"Your dad looks great."

"Yeah, but take a look at his mother. There's a real possibility I could look like her in forty years. And much as I love her, I don't want her body. She's an apple."

"If it's any consolation, my grandmother is shaped like a pear," Megan said. "Hate to say it, but, apple, pear, I think we're all headed there someday."

"You're probably right," I replied. "Obviously there's a reason they named those apples after Granny Smith and not her husband."

"Forget all that," Bree said. "You're a successful woman in charge of her life—and today you really look like it. So go get 'em!"

I let out a nervous laugh. "Okay, see you inside."

I shut off my phone and drove slowly through the parking lot searching for a spot that was far enough from the door to be discreet, yet not so far that the journey would be torture in Jen's black, patent leather-trimmed spike heels. Nerves bouncing like a high-strung Chihuahua, I pushed open my car door, took hold of my sister's wonderful, tote-style, soft red leather Coach briefcase, and began to stride purposely across the blacktopped parking lot—well, as purposely as one can stride against a headwind in a black, knee-length pencil skirt and stilettos.

By the time I reached the hotel's side door, my heart was thudding wildly. *We were doing this thing. We were actually doing it.* The Continental Breakfast Club was about to go live. I confidently grasped the door handle and pulled.

It didn't budge.

A thin reed of panic streaked up my core. I tamped it down and reminded myself this wasn't an unexpected development; we'd known in advance the door would be locked. All I had to do was wait for someone to come out... or go in. I released the handle, adopted an unconcerned manner, and pivoted to gaze nonchalantly over the cars in the parking lot. My attention settled momentarily on my silver Civic, then slid to Megan's black Camry, inside which she and Bree were doing a stellar job of appearing to be two women chatting away, totally unaware of anything around them.

The wind swirled my hair and I smoothed some

strands off my forehead, then brushed imaginary lint from the front of my beautiful skirt. Pride skittered through me. I really was lucky that Jen had such an eye for fashion.

Determined to look like a legitimate hotel guest, I began to root through my briefcase as though I might actually find a key if I searched hard enough. Nervously, I tugged up on the low neckline of my white blouse, then straightened my belt, letting my palm slip over the indentation of my waist. I may be a few pounds overweight but I was no apple yet.

I squinted at the hotel door again, and my stomach took a flop. What if no one used this door? What if it was only for emergencies or deliveries? *What if the manager came out and accused me of loitering?*

I took a step toward my car, ready to abandon the plan and flee to the safety of my friends. And then I remembered what was at stake—the respect of my entire family.

In a month I would be twenty-eight. Twenty-eight years of being told what to do. Twenty-eight years of being left out of family decisions. Twenty-eight years of never-ending child-status.

I set my shoulders and tried some biofeedback to settle my nerves. Breathing deeply, I reminded myself that just a few days ago Bree had test-entered the hotel through this very door, no problem. I pictured the scene inside: eligible bachelors drinking coffee, eating sweet rolls, having their omelets made just the way they wanted. And among them might be the man who would change my life—a successful man, a handsome man, a man who would adore me enough to marry me and, thus, launch me to adulthood in my family's eyes.

Whew. Tall order, I know. But if I was going to dream, I might as well dream big.

I began to rummage through my briefcase again, the way someone would if she were really stuck outside the hotel and couldn't find her key. Sweat beaded on my shoulders.

"Come on," I muttered under my breath as I willed the door to open. When it didn't obey my command, I made a snap decision to take a risk and try the main entrance. As I strolled toward the front of the building, I heard the crunchy squeak of a heavy door opening. Glancing over my shoulder, I spotted a man in a tan linen suit exiting the hotel.

I pivoted so fast on my sister's stilettos, I nearly twisted an ankle. "Ho-hold the—" I choked out, dashing back the way I'd come.

The man was talking on a cell phone and oblivious to my presence until I rocketed past him and snagged the door just before it latched shut. Interrupted mid-sentence, he blinked, mouth open and speechless, as though this interaction was well outside his norm at six-thirty in the morning and it was too early to figure out how to respond.

"Sorry. Forgot my key," I said on an exhale as I jerked the door open and stepped inside.

The door clunked shut with prison-like finality. I

grinned. Success! We had done it. Pulse hammering, I spun slowly to take in my surroundings. *Subdued elegance* would have to be the phrase of the day. Rich hues covered the walls, the carpet, the furniture. No doubt the shades and colors had evocative names like summer lawn, warm toast, spring fog, and whitecap.

A mahogany half-round table rested beneath an oval, gilt-framed mirror. On each side, a plush leather chair invited me to sink down and relax. The air was quiet and still, as though sound was instantly absorbed, swallowed up before it could disturb the guests.

The effect of all this sophistication sent a ripple of excitement through me. There'd be no riff-raff in this hotel; the men would most certainly be of the high caliber we sought.

I stepped forward to take a quick appraisal of myself in the mirror, turning slightly left and right to make sure that not one iota of *doggg groooomer* was peeking out anywhere. My makeup was soft and natural. And I'd put extra effort into my hair—instead of my usual ponytail, I'd followed the directions online for a windswept chignon. Unfortunately, my windswept chignon appeared to have gone through a tornado—blame it on the breezy day and a little too much prep spray. I smoothed it down with my hands and tried to stick the loose ends back into place. After a minute, I gave up. It would have to do.

I still looked quite pulled together, tailored yet fashionable, the epitome of a successful woman on a business trip.

Sales trip, actually. *"I'm in pet nutrition for a dog food manufacturer,"* I mentally recited, glad I'd chosen a profession somewhat related to my real job. At least I'd be able to lie halfway believably. *"I sell specialty dog food to veterinarians and wholesalers. Yes, it's quite lucrative."*

I pictured myself across the breakfast table from a handsome executive wearing a dark gray suit, white button-down shirt, and blue tie. He would have two pieces of toast, buttered, and a cup of black coffee, steaming. *"Will you be in town long?"* he'd ask. I would sip my orange juice and let out a light, sparkly laugh. *"Just a few days to call on some key accounts. How about you?"* Our gazes would meet. *"I'll be here a few days also,"* he'd say in a deep, sultry voice. I would reach gracefully across the table to touch his wrist—

"Excuse me," a male voice said.

In the span of a heartbeat, my gray-suited fantasy evaporated and I saw myself through a stranger's eyes: a woman flirting with her own reflection. *Call the management; she's not one of us.*

Self-preservation kicked in, and I moved to the side and pretended to brush something off the surface of the mirror so my behavior might seem perfectly normal. He passed without acknowledging me, towing a black, wheeled suitcase behind him as he disappeared around the corner. Obviously he thought I was just another guest at the hotel. Excitement tap danced through me. *I belonged!*

I returned to the door and pushed it open to let Megan

and Bree inside. "Nice outfits, girls." I nodded approvingly at their business attire.

Bree led the way to the ladies lounge—an elegant space furnished with a plush navy print sofa and two over-stuffed chairs. After a quick inspection confirmed we were alone, we got down to business.

"Breakfast is probably in full swing now," Megan said. "Any last minute questions? Are you ready, Allie?"

Palms damp, I faced myself in the mirror. *Was I?* "As I'll ever be, I guess."

"Okay. Bree will follow you out in five minutes. And I'll be right here if either of you need me." Megan reached out to straighten my blouse. "Just remember. Act like you belong—"

"And you belong." I lifted my chin, straightened my shoulders, and set off for the breakfast room.

While I waited for my oversized waffle to cook, I surreptitiously checked out the faces and ring fingers of the men in the room. Too old, too odd, too young, too old, too old, too young, too flashy, not bad—oooh, the sandy blonde-haired guy at the corner table reading the New York Times and drinking coffee...now he might be worth breakfasting with. If only his left hand wasn't under the newspaper.

Luckily for Bree and me, there were plenty of businessmen in the room—of every shape, size, and age.

Unfortunately, there were also two open tables, which created a definite problem. Why would I need to share a table with a complete stranger when I could have one of the empties to myself? The only solution was to postpone taking a seat until all the tables were taken. Which is why I was making a waffle; the process guaranteed me at least a few minutes of waiting.

The beeper went off on the waffle machine just as a man and woman sat at one of the open tables. Heartened, I sent up a silent prayer for someone else to quickly take the other empty table, then continued stalling by putting half an English muffin in the toaster and adding other food to my tray. The donut platter slid into my peripheral vision and I scrutinized its contents. Was that a chocolate-frosted, custard-filled donut?

I swallowed. My hand almost reached out of its own accord, my fingers actually twitched. But I already had almost a mountain of food—a steaming waffle slathered in butter and syrup, an English muffin slathered in strawberry jam, a half bagel slathered in cream cheese, a blueberry muffin slathered in honey—and I didn't want my potential new love to think I wasn't health conscious. After all, I'd been exercising at the gym for the past month. The donut would have to wait. Hopefully anyone I met would think I was merely ravenous, not gluttonous.

As an older woman took the last empty table in the room, I added a few chunks of pineapple and cantaloupe to my plate for good measure, poured myself a mug of coffee and a small orange juice, then turned to peruse the room—and the available men—one more time.

New York Times was still there, and definitely luscious. Clean cut and classic, he was dressed to the nines in a gray suit—exactly the type of man I'd been visualizing in my admittedly adolescent daydreaming. But just a few tables away, a close second had sneaked into the room and was checking his iPhone. Dashingly dangerous in a dark sport coat and charcoal slacks, he had thick brown hair and a day's growth on his jaw—definitely not the image of the typical businessman. Plus, he clearly wasn't wearing a wedding ring. That made him a bird-in-the-hand, while New York Times, with his ring finger concealed beneath the paper, remained an unknown.

The girls and I had planned to use today as a practice run, but what if one of these guys was *the one who was meant to be*? I just couldn't walk away from the possibility. Oh God, what to do? iPhone versus New York Times. Dashingly dangerous versus clean cut and classic. Bird-in-the-hand versus two in the bush. How did I choose? We hadn't even discussed such a scenario during planning.

I drew a slow breath and ordered myself to hurry up. If I stood there frozen much longer, the tables would empty out again and I'd be back to square one. So, I quickly set a rating standard...which man would I rather wake up beside for the rest of my life?

I pictured New York Times in the morning, his hair tousled, his eyes heavily lidded with sleep. To tell the truth, I'd never dated anyone as attractive as New York Times. And I just knew my family would love him.

Take the gamble, I told myself. Gripping my food-laden tray with white fingers, I walked over to New York Times and asked, "Excuse me, do you mind if I take this seat?" I looked around the room as though making a last-ditch effort to find my own table. "It's pretty crowded in here this morning."

He glanced up in surprise and grinned, his smile so dazzling, his teeth so white, my breath actually caught. "Sure," he said.

Oh dear God, my brain whispered, please let him be single.

As he pulled his newspaper back to make room at the table, his left hand came into view. Unadorned. Unmarried. *Jackpot!*

No way was this a practice run. I could feel it. This was him, he, *the one who was meant to be.* Wait until I told Megan and Bree. Wait until my family met him. Oh, the life we would have together—filled with love, joy and beautiful children!

I slid into the seat opposite and curved my lips demurely upward. Good thing he had no idea there was a dance party going on in my brain.

THREE

FROM THE CORNER OF MY EYE, I SPOTTED BREE HEADING FOR the buffet counter. Though neither of us publicly acknowledged the other, Bree dipped her chin as she passed and I knew she was giving me kudos for how well I had landed.

A feeling of invincibility filled me and I gazed pleasantly across the table at my New York Times man. "Crowded in here today," I said.

"It always is this early."

I gave a sparkly laugh and took a sip of juice. This was amazing. I was almost living my daydream to the letter. "So you stay here often?" I tucked a tiny bite of syrup-drenched waffle into my mouth, and for the first time in my life found the sweetness nauseating. This was not good. I was too nervous to eat, and I had a lot of food to get through.

He folded his newspaper and smiled again. A zing shot

through my chest and I thought it could be nothing short of a piercing by cupid's arrow.

"First time, actually," he said. "I just meant that hotel breakfasts are always busy early in the morning."

"Oh, right, I know." I took another bite of waffle and searched for something to say, but all the conversation starters I'd practiced with Bree and Megan had disappeared into a black hole. I chewed slowly, then swallowed the soggy, syrup-saturated lump. "This is my first time staying here, too." *Clever, very clever.* I was such a natural conversationalist.

"Usually my partner and I stay at the Dalton but it was full."

Partner? The man was a lawyer! Or maybe he owned a business! Either way, he had to be successful if his usual hotel was the Dalton Inn, an expensive and elegant renovated mansion, generally considered among the most upscale in town.

I took a bite of my English muffin and sneaked another glance his way. Handsome, well-dressed, and surely intelligent—as a general rule, dimwits didn't usually get too far in the self-employed arena.

He took a drink of his coffee—black—and I noticed his cup was nearly empty. That was my warning to get the conversation going or he'd soon be on his way out of the breakfast room and this relationship would be on its way to nowhere.

"Where are you from?" I ventured.

"L.A." He raised a hand in greeting to another man who had just stepped into the dining room.

"Your partner?" I asked.

He nodded, eyes still on the other man.

What luck! The one was as gorgeous and well-dressed as the other. If only there were some way I could introduce the partner to Bree. Maybe we could have a double date. Or a double wedding! What were the odds that we would find these two perfect—

My thoughts broke off as New York Times tilted his head...coyly. My brow furrowed. The men exchanged a look, *a lingering look*. I'd seen that expression before, had taken part in such intimate exchanges myself.

That's when I knew, even before I knew. My mood began to sink. No, no, no, this couldn't be happening. New York Times turned his luminous smile back to me as he folded his newspaper and picked up his coffee cup. "Have a great day," he said. Then he walked across the room to brush fingertips with his partner before they rounded the corner into the lobby and out of my sight.

What were the odds? Handsome, rich, well-dressed, undoubtedly intelligent...and gay. Just my luck.

I jammed another chunk of waffle into my mouth. The syrup dripped down my chin and I didn't even care. Not only had I chosen the wrong guy, but now I had zero chances of meeting anyone else because there was no way I could leap to my feet and switch tables—barring, of course, a major spill of some sort. And I really wasn't up to that level of theatrics. I searched for Bree and found her talking and laughing at a table with *two* successful-looking men.

Humph. I tromped miserably over to the donut table to claim the last chocolate-frosted, custard-filled, fat and carbohydrate-loaded gem on the tray. If manhunting was over for the morning, I might as well enjoy a little high blood sugar.

Back at my table, I stretched out in my chair and closed my eyes slightly to fully enjoy the rich conglomeration of flavors—the creamy filling, the moist cake surround, the buttery chocolate frosting, the delectable deliciousness of—

A quitter never wins and a winner never quits. My lids popped open and I sat up. Really? In the midst of my misery, my mother was going to invade my thoughts with her favorite motivational quote? If I'd heard it once, I'd heard it a thousand times—especially with regard to vet school.

I grudgingly acknowledged that giving up wouldn't help me find a man who would deliver the respect I wanted from my family. Breakfast was still young and there was plenty of time before the first dogs would be dropped at Flawless Paws, so why not leave for a few minutes and try again? With so many people coming and going in the room, it was unlikely that anyone would even notice I'd filled a tray once already. Standing, I casually dumped my food in the garbage can in the corner, deposited my dishes in the bus tub, and slipped down the hall to the ladies lounge.

"Down, but not out," Megan proclaimed when I told her what happened. "You're absolutely right. No one will remember you. They're all in their own worlds. By the time you go back in, the room will probably be full of all new breakfasters. New choices will abound."

The fact that her response agreed with mine gave me even greater confidence.

"Allie, just remember," she said, "today is only a practice run."

Practice be damned. I was in it to win.

Back in the breakfast room, the first thing I noticed was that all the tables were taken. Good. I grabbed a plate and a tray, hurriedly took a thick slice of banana bread and a scoop of fresh fruit, and poured myself a cup of coffee and an orange juice while surreptitiously perusing the available men. This time around I would be less particular.

My eyes skipped from one man to the next. Too old, too young, too old, too casual, too—stop! *Too picky.* I swung my gaze back to Too Casual, even though he wasn't dressed anything like the man in my daydreams. Instead of a gray suit, he was wearing jeans and a blue-striped, long-sleeved shirt cuffed up at the wrists. But he had a strong jaw and broad shoulders and his black hair was a bit on the longish side. He looked tough and polished at the same time, and I wouldn't have been surprised to learn he was an executive at a successful dot com. He scanned the room like he was bored, half-smiling at me before his gaze moved on.

I had to admit, he was the visual epitome of the handsome bad boy. So, while he might not perfectly fit my gray-suited fantasy of *the one who was meant to be,* I figured he might be worth a practice run. Decision made, I put on a friendly front, ignored my jittery stomach, and made my move. "Is there room at your table this lovely morning?" I asked.

God save me from myself, did I really say *this lovely morning?*

He looked back at me through two beautiful, dark gray eyes. Black hair, charcoal eyes, chiseled jaw. What a gorgeous combination. "Room for one more," he said, grinning, which seemed a bit odd, but I could hardly be critical when I'd just said something formal and bizarre in a weak attempt at clever and appealing.

As I set my tray on the table and slid into a chair, I noticed his breakfast choices. Toast, coffee, and a sweet roll. Healthy, but not a health freak. Thank God I had gone with lighter fare this time around.

"I'm Allie," I said, extending a hand across the table. "Thanks for sharing."

He hesitated a moment before taking my hand. "Colin Hughes."

"Sounds like an Irish movie star," I quipped.

His brows drew together like he wasn't sure how to respond. Silence rolled over us and I scrambled to do damage control. "I mean Irish movie star in a good way, a leading man sort of way, a strong, memorable, Academy-Award-winning way." What the hell was I babbling to a complete stranger? I gave a feeble laugh. "So now that we've established you're not in the movies, what brings you here?" I took a bite of toast so I would be forced to stop talking. *Please, please, please,* I implored the universe, *don't let me have messed this up.*

He hesitated, and my mind went into overdrive. Did he think I was unhinged? Nosy? Desperate? Then he bent forward like we were conspirators and said, "Jewelry. Gems. Whatever customers are looking for, I...source it." He smiled a little smugly. "I'm the...CEO of the Intercontinental Jewelry Exchange." he quipped.

CEO of the Intercontinental Jewelry Exchange? Omigod, maybe I could amaze and astonish my parents after all.

"Oh, yes," I said, bobbing my head as though I'd heard of the organization before. I wasn't too worried about telling a little white lie; one quick Internet search on my phone and I would probably learn everything I needed to know about his company in minutes. "Emeralds and rubies..."

"And diamonds. We specialize in diamonds."

"A girl's best friend," I trilled giddily, convinced that Colin might be the perfect choice for my parents' anniversary party. Handsome, an international businessman, clearly an upper-crust kind of guy. If this worked out, I'd be promoted to adult in the family's eyes in no time.

"I think they're everyone's best friend, don't you?" He almost seemed to be studying me.

I flustered under his scrutiny. Was he flirting? At breakfast?

"I don't see you wearing any." I fluttered my lashes at the bare ring finger of his left hand and gave him a coquettish smile. Wow, I never acted like this.

"I don't like to flaunt it."

"Of course," I said, even though I didn't actually know what he meant. He didn't like bling? He didn't like to flaunt his status as a married man? Oh God, don't tell me Colin was married. I took a drink of juice and tried to figure out how to get to the bottom of his marital status.

"It makes perfect sense," I said slowly. "Some people might be put off by bling, or a...flashy wedding ring. If you look too prosperous, they may start to wonder if your prices are fair—"

The corners of his mouth curved downward.

"I mean," I blabbered on, knowing I should shut up and quit making assumptions, "you don't want to appear to be taking advantage of buyers, it might...stop them from doing business with you." I sneaked a glance over at Bree and her two men. Seemed like things were going swimmingly over there.

When Colin didn't reply, I opened my mouth to start talking again, as though more words would untie the knot I had gotten myself into. Before I could even get started, he let out a laugh. "First, I'm not married. And second, you don't have to worry about my prices. I'm known for being *very* fair. I have a lot of repeat customers." He paused a moment. "As much as I'd like to give out references, though, it's not a good idea in my line of work."

"Oh, absolutely, I'm sure."

"I don't flaunt it because it makes people take notice," he said carefully. "Invites questions. I work in relative anonymity to protect both me and my customers."

I remembered an article I'd read about gangs of thieves that targeted jewelry manufacturers' sales reps. The reps discovered that the best way to protect themselves from getting robbed was to dress down—wear jeans and base-ball caps, and carry their samples in duffle bags instead of leather cases. Suddenly Colin's answers and attire made perfect sense.

"It's about being less conspicuous," I said.

"Exactly." He popped the last bite of his sweet roll into his mouth and licked the icing from the tip of his index finger. I could have swooned.

This guy was fascinating. I could see my family gathered around him on the patio, captivated, with me next to him, proud and content. My sister would ask, *"Allie, with so many thieves everywhere, don't you worry all the time?"* And I would gently touch Colin's knee and reply, *"Yes, but such is the life he's chosen, and so it is my choice, too."* He would place his hand over mine and I would lean into him, connecting us, that simple movement showing the depth of our love—

"So, what do you think?" Colin drained his coffee cup.

Think? About what? I'd gotten so caught up in my daydream, I'd actually zoned out for a minute. What had I missed? I gave a noncommittal smile and scrolled back through as much of the conversation as I could remember, searching for a clue. Good God, I couldn't tell *the one who was meant to be* that I hadn't been listening.

"Oh, I think that..." I quickly shoved a chunk of banana bread into my mouth, then held up one finger to indicate I would answer as soon as I'd swallowed it down. What I planned to say was anyone's guess.

I surveyed the room in desperation, spotting Bree looking at me sideways and lightly tapping the back of her wrist. *Time?* My brain somersaulted. I peeked at my watch and almost had a coronary. A golden retriever was being dropped off at Flawless Paws for a bath and comb out in less than half an hour. Not being there when he arrived wasn't even an option; I needed every customer I could get. At least it would give me a reason to escape without having to admit I hadn't been listening.

I shoved back my chair and stood. "I'm so sorry. I just realized I'm about to be late for an appointment."

He blinked. "O-kay."

From across the room, Bree dipped her chin and I knew that was code for *Ask him. Ask him. Ask him.* The question was, could I? Did I have it in me? Could I really ask Colin to get together again?

I gazed into his beautiful charcoal eyes and decided to go for broke. After all, what did I have to lose? "I'd love to hear more about your jewels..." *His jewels?* Seriously? Had I just said that? The words felt like they'd come from someone else's mouth.

Colin stood without answering. My nerves danced. My stomach lurched. There was no way I could go through with this. No way. It didn't matter that I'd never see him again if he said *no*, didn't matter that no one would ever find out I had even asked the question. Nope, I could not go through with—

And then my mouth began to move by itself. "Maybe we could get together again and you could tell me more..."

Surprise flitted across his face.

Self-conscious heat shot through me. I didn't know what I would do if he said, *Are you asking me on a date?*

Because my answer would have to be something like, *Oh, no, I just want to learn about your business.* Except that would be a totally stupid response because I *was* asking him on a date. So actually, what I should say was, *"Well, yes, I am—"*

Brow furrowed, Colin took a quick perusal of the breakfast room before settling his gaze back on me. "Later tonight?"

Tonight? Wow, this guy didn't let any grass grow under his feet. I picked up Jen's briefcase and mentally raced through the day's schedule. If all the pet owners arrived on time, I'd be free by six o'clock. I'd need to run home to beautify—reapply makeup and fix my hair. Should I wear the clothes I had on or go more casual? Jen's outfit made me feel so confident, I really wanted to wear it again. So, I would. I'd just tell Colin I'd come straight from calling on one of my dog food customers—

"How about seven-thirty?" Colin finally asked when I took too long to reply.

I flushed, embarrassed. "Sure. That would be perfect."

"Great, I'll buy you a drink to seal it."

Drinks! We'd just leapfrogged over latte at the local coffee house. Plus the bar at Tucker Point would be private, drastically reducing the odds I would run into anyone I knew who might blow my cover. "Sure," I said too brightly. "Sounds great," I added in a more subdued voice.

Wait. What did he want to seal? What could we seal? A deal? What deal? *Our love?* Oh, for God's sake. We'd just met—obviously he couldn't be talking about *love.* I felt a shiver of trepidation; concern seeped into my excitement. So what was he—?

"There's a place downtown that I like," he said before I could ask what we were sealing. "Out of the way. Sullivan's. Ever been there?"

Shit. So much for privacy at the hotel bar. Sullivan's was a very happening Irish pub frequented by self-impressed, up-and-comers. Not the worst choice, I guessed. If we had to meet in public, Sullivan's was one place where I could probably be guaranteed not to see anyone I knew.

"Never heard of it, but I can get directions online," I

lied. My pulse had begun to dance, my legs to tremble. This was happening awfully fast.

"Great, see you tonight." Colin stuck out a hand and we shook on it. Kind of an unusual way to set up a date, but clearly, Colin wasn't an average guy.

"Tonight," I said because I didn't think I could get a full sentence out without my voice quivering. Then I turned as gracefully as I could on those skinny black heels and charged down the hall to the ladies restroom.

Megan shot off the couch the moment I came through the door. "How'd it go?"

I let out a laugh. Even cool, calm, and collected Megan couldn't contain herself this morning. I rattled off my story leaving out the slight reservations I was having. Megan brought her hands together in a celebratory clap. "Sullivan's? He wants to meet you at Sullivan's? The man knows his restaurants," she said gleefully. "*I am so good.* Now, if Bree's got good news—"

"No good news." Bree stepped into the room shaking her head.

"But you had *two* guys. Both cute," I said. "You were having a great time. I saw you. I heard you. If there'd been any more hilarity at your table, I'd have thought you had a laugh track."

She sighed and dropped onto the couch. "I know. It was wonderful. I couldn't decide which one I liked better. Just as I was working up the courage to say, *let's do this again,* one of them said they were flying back to Nebraska this afternoon."

"Prospects leaving town is a definite downside to this method." Megan sat next to Bree and gave her knee a pat. "But on a brighter note, you did meet eligible men. And tomorrow is another day."

"I don't know. It was pretty stressful." Bree wrinkled her nose. "How'd you do, Allie?"

"We're meeting for drinks tonight."

Bree leapt to her feet with a strangled scream. "The second guy, right? I knew it!" Arms in the air, she did a happy dance. "Okay, I'm totally renewed. Tell me everything."

"His name is Colin Hughes. He's the CEO of the Intercontinental Jewelry Exchange."

"Oh. My. God. Handsome *and* successful. Double bonus for you." She let out a laugh. "Are you ecstatic?"

I made a face. "Maybe. I don't know...it really happened so fast."

"And that's bad?" Bree let out a chortle. "Obviously you two hit it off. Stop over-analyzing—go out and have fun."

"It's just drinks," Megan added. "Not marriage, God forbid."

Yeah, they were right. I should live in the moment. Just because this guy was eager to see me again didn't mean he was a serial killer or something.

Bree waved a hand. "So tell us more."

"Later," I said heading for the door. "If I don't get to the shop before my clients arrive, I'm not going to have a business anymore."

"Okay, but let me say this right now," Bree shot back, grinning. "I know I wasn't at your table, but from what I could see, I don't think you're going to find anything wrong with that man."

FOUR

Later that night, I stepped through the front door of Sullivan's, excited and nervous, dressed in the outfit I'd been wearing at continental breakfast. Thank God I'd been able to find a parking space right outside; Jen's stilettos were still as precarious to walk in as they'd been that morning.

After a quick discussion at home, Bree and I decided the best way to prevent Colin from discovering holes in my weak cover story was to make sure he didn't have a chance to ask too many questions. Of course we knew that if the relationship started to go somewhere, the truth was going to have to come out eventually. But our short-term goal was to make sure that discussion took place *after* the first date. Which meant, my immediate goal for the evening was to keep Colin talking.

I spotted him almost immediately at a cozy table in the

corner next to a dark wood-paneled wall. He seemed so right sitting there, a black-haired Irishman in an Irish bar with a pint of ale in front of him. I wiped my damp palms on the sides of Jen's skirt—what she didn't know wouldn't hurt her—and headed across the restaurant. Colin smiled and raised his glass in greeting. He didn't stand, but then, why quibble over formalities?

"Did you have any trouble finding the place?" he asked.

At least I didn't have to lie about that. "No, it was easy. GPS is so helpful. How did we ever get along without it?" I took the seat to his left and hung my purse over the back of the chair.

One glass of cabernet later, which I downed rather quickly, and my jitters had been sanded smooth. I probably should have ordered Guinness or Smithwick's or something Gaelic-sounding since my date had an Irish name and we were in an Irish bar and I wanted to impress him, but I knew wine would be the fastest way to take the edge off my nerves.

After a couple of minutes of amiable small talk, my worries of the morning vanished. Colin really seemed to be the total package—even more charming and handsome than he'd been that morning. The rich resonance of his voice made me want to listen to him talk forever. Plus, there was that international jewelry job of his.

As if reading my mind, he said, "You asked about gems this morning. I specialize in diamonds, in maintaining a unique inventory. New things are coming in all the time.

Are you thinking of something specific or would you just like a general overview?" His eyes roamed the restaurant for a few seconds.

I waved a breezy hand and forced a smile, reluctant to admit that my question at breakfast had been nothing more than a nervous mistake. "Oh, just, you know, in general would be fine." Then, because that almost sounded like I wasn't very interested, I asked, "Do you also source gems in Europe?" so he would have plenty to talk about.

He didn't respond, just looked past me as though preoccupied, one finger tapping absently on the table. I cleared my throat and he sharpened his gaze on me again. There was a subtle disquiet about him tonight, something I couldn't quite put my finger on. I hoped he wasn't already having second thoughts about me. Maybe he just wasn't used to dating—that would explain a lot.

"Not just Europe," he finally replied. "All over the world. The interest in beautiful gems and jewelry is widespread. Many of my clients view gems as an investment. Not unlike buying a fine painting."

That was the moment the reality of our match-up sunk in. Gem expert. *Doggg groooomer.* He could never find out. *Never.*

Okay, fine, that was probably an unrealistic expectation. But at least I could keep him from learning I was a dog groomer until he was so madly in love with me he didn't care that my job paled next to his.

"Wow!" I said, mortified that my vocabulary seemed to have frozen at the fifth grade level. "I'm not surprised. It makes sense you would be well-connected."

"Relationships are important in my business. Trust helps me move stock quickly and discretely."

I nodded. He really did seem perfect. I couldn't wait for my parents to see what a great guy I'd landed. A quiet alarm bell went off in the back of my brain, one of those warnings about things that seem too good to be true, usually are. I ignored it. After all, I reasoned, Colin certainly hadn't gone to breakfast on a quest to meet a woman. I'd been the one to approach him, not the other way around.

He shifted in his seat, eyes roving the restaurant again. His distractedness was kind of unsettling, but I was determined to give him the benefit of the doubt. After a moment, he took a swallow of beer and leaned toward me across the table. "Do you mind if we fast-forward to the important questions?"

My heart skittered, my thoughts went crazy. What important questions? *Ever married? Engaged? Children? Love?* Surely, he wasn't going to talk about love already? I'd heard of love at first sight but never experienced it myself, and while I was sure I didn't love him yet, who knew what he might be feeling."

"Sure, absolutely." I took several quick sips of wine to steel my courage. Hopefully we wouldn't start talking about where our families lived. Or where I lived. Or where we should live together, for that matter. Oh my God. *Stop.*

Colin waited expectantly.

What? He wanted me to go first? I didn't even know what his definition of *important questions* was. My body temperature began to rise and my thoughts began to scatter...more than they usually did anyway. I needed to ask something that didn't seem too forward, that made me seem interesting and intriguing, that was *important.* Except, every question I came up with made me sound like a gold digger. Finally I blurted, "Is yours a family business?"

Colin's brow furrowed like he was working through a difficult problem, and I couldn't tell if he didn't know how to answer my question or hadn't actually heard me. After a moment, he swiped his phone to check his messages.

His brow furrowed with concern. "I'm sorry, I need to return a call. An important customer in Zurich and... I may need to go there soon." He tapped two fingers on the tabletop. "The signal in here is terrible—I don't even have one bar." He pushed back his chair and stood. "Be back in a minute."

Moments later, the waitress arrived with the appetizer we'd ordered—baked goat cheese on Irish brown bread. I asked for another cabernet, texted Megan and Bree that everything was going great, then sat back feeling awesome in my sophisticated clothes. I couldn't help noticing there were plenty of male glances coming my way. If this thing didn't work out with Colin, maybe I'd borrow Jen's clothes again and come back to Sullivan's another time.

I nibbled at the appetizers, feeling sorry for Colin that he had to deal with customer problems at night. It probably had to do with the time zones; maybe it was already the next workday in Switzerland.

I looked up the world time clock on my phone to check the time in Zurich. It was the middle of the night. Weird. But what did I know about the gem business? Maybe there'd been a jewel heist or something. The thought gave me a little thrill. After all, something as exciting as a jewel heist would never be an issue in my business.

After Colin had been gone ten minutes, I was still feeling sorry for him, but I was also getting bored. And ravenous. I'd hardly eaten any dinner because of nerves. Stage fright, you could almost call it, because I was certainly acting up a storm.

Finally, I quit holding back and dug into the appetizers in earnest. They were so fabulous, I wolfed down every morsel, and then, horrified that Colin would come back and see I'd devoured everything, placed a second order and asked the waitress to rush it. When that platter arrived, I quickly ate a couple more so when Colin returned he wouldn't think I was some weirdo who refused to eat any of the appetizers while he was away from the table.

By the time half an hour passed, I began to worry that something had gone wrong outside—maybe he'd had a heart attack or been mugged. If I had his cell phone number I could have called him, but we'd never exchanged numbers because I left continental breakfast in such a rush.

So I threw my purse over my shoulder and went outside on a search and rescue mission. As I walked the parking lot, toes pinched and skinny heels wobbling over every uneven patch of asphalt, two guys made passes at me. Which was slightly awkward because I already had a date—even though he was missing in action.

I started shining my phone flashlight into car windows, hoping to spot Colin inside his car; problem was, I had no idea what kind of car he had. Unfortunately, all I ended up doing was illuminating a half-undressed couple, making out, who were not amused to be exposed by my bright white beam. As the guy shouted at me and struggled to pull his pants up, I escaped back into the restaurant, quickly deciding not to check any of the cars parked on the street. I wasn't going to cross the line from *concerned date* to *peeping Tom* to *stalker* by peering into every car in a two block radius. Even I had my limits.

Discouraged, I dropped my purse on the floor by my chair and finished off the rest of the appetizers. I would have ordered another glass of wine just to drown my sorrows, but the waistband of Jen's skirt was now so tight it was hard to draw a full breath. Besides, I had to drive home.

The waitress set the bill on the table and that's when it

hit me. Colin had used that phone call to ditch me. I'd been deserted. Publicly. And left to pick up the tab.

I went from caring date, to embarrassed cast-off, to angry spurned women in the course of five seconds. Apparently, the *important questions* Colin had been referring to included, *Are you so desperate for a guy that you'll let yourself get stuck with the bill?*

Apparently the answer was *yes*.

The double order of appetizers I'd gobbled down swirled in my belly. I sat there, motionless, for a minute, trying to breathe without popping the top button off my skirt. Then, knowing I had no other choices, I bent to retrieve my purse from under the table. And spotted a briefcase. Hardsided dark brown leather, slightly scuffed, in the shadows along the wall next to Colin's chair.

It had to be his. Had. To. Be. Had. Had. Had. To. Be.

Hope flared anew. Colin certainly wouldn't have run for the hills without his briefcase.

Unless, in his rush to get away from me, he'd simply forgotten he brought his briefcase. Hope morphed back into anger.

I considered leaving the briefcase for someone else to find—or better yet, steal. It would serve him right for disappearing on me. On the other hand, what if he had a good excuse? What if I left his briefcase behind only to learn later that something unimaginable had happened? Then I would feel awful if the case had gone missing. Deciding I should probably give Colin the benefit of the doubt, I lifted the attaché onto the chair next to me and pushed the metal tabs on the top edge so I could get inside the thing and find his phone number.

Locked.

Of course. It made perfect sense. The guy ran the Intercontinental Jewelry Exchange, after all. The case was probably full of all sorts of important information for his job. Maybe even expensive jewelry.

Understanding why it was locked didn't make me feel any better, though. I irritably swiped open my phone and Googled both the Intercontinental Jewelry Exchange (no listing) and Colin Hughes (trillions of listings). My breath hissed out sharply from between my teeth.

Even if it turned out that Colin hadn't run out on me, even if something unimaginable had happened, it didn't negate the fact that I'd been sitting in the restaurant alone for almost an hour, that I'd gotten stuck with the bill, that my feet hurt and my waistband was now agonizingly tight.

I wanted to go home.

Tossing enough cash on the table to cover the bill and a tip, I slung my purse over my shoulder, wrapped both arms around the briefcase, and strode from the restaurant. I no longer cared that I looked like a million bucks in Jen's clothes. I no longer reveled in the second glances I was getting. I just wanted to get home, lick my wounds, and get the fuck out of those shoes.

I threw the briefcase in the backseat of my car and sped away, taking satisfaction in leaving Sullivan's—and the evening—in the dust. Halfway home, I pulled over to call the Tucker Point Hotel and leave a message for Colin. The desk clerk seemed perplexed. "We have no reservation for Colin Hughes or the Intercontinental Jewelry Exchange," she said. "Could it be under another name?"

Certainly it could. No doubt it was. He'd probably registered incognito because of jewelry theft gangs, but I couldn't say that to her without giving away his cover. "Can I leave a message just in case he stops at the desk?" I asked desperately.

I knew the odds of him checking in at the front desk were probably low, but I couldn't think of anything else to do. When she agreed, I gave her Colin's name again, dictated a message that he could pick up the briefcase the next day at Flawless Paws, and rattled off the address and my cell phone number.

Then I called Bree and Megan on a three-way to fill them in.

"Maybe there's a totally legit reason he didn't come back right away," Bree said. "A fire in a diamond mine or something."

"Yeah, that sounds like a totally legit reason," Megan deadpanned.

I ignored them. "I tried to find a phone number on the Internet, but there were zero hits for the Intercontinental Jewelry Exchange. There's not even a website. And the hotel doesn't have a reservation for him or his company."

Bree tsked. "Not everyone wants to be all over the Internet, you know."

"People who are followed and robbed and murdered by jewelry thieves might especially want to be hard to find," Megan added.

I was relieved to hear that their logic mirrored mine. "That's what I thought, too. So I left a message at the front desk with my phone number and said I'd have the brief-case at Flawless Paws tomorrow."

"You left your work address?" Bree asked, horrified. "Are you cracked? If he shows up at Flawless Paws, he's going to know right away that you're not what you said you are. Goodbye true love."

My body temperature skyrocketed. Like I was combusting. "Can't I just say I'm doing in-service training there? He thinks I'm a dog food sales rep. He wouldn't have any idea if that's part of the job or not."

"It's believable enough," Megan said. I could practi-cally see her nodding, which made my tension begin to ease. "But, if he doesn't call tonight," she continued, "just go back to continental breakfast tomorrow so you can run into him and give his briefcase back before he ever shows up at the shop. Go early—"

"And stay late," Bree added. "You don't want to miss him."

The next morning I slid into a persimmon-colored sheath of Jen's, teamed it with her fabulous nude heels, and arrived at breakfast right when it opened. I poured myself a cup of coffee, got a piece of toast, and collected a complimentary copy of USA Today from the magazine rack. The not-eating part was easy since I'd single-handedly finished off two full orders of Irish brown bread and goat cheese not very many hours ago. I settled in to wait, somewhat apprehensive, but sure that once I heard Colin's rational explanation, everything would be fine.

I pictured seeing him again. "You were gone so long," I would say. "I wasn't sure what to do." He'd run a worried hand through his thick hair. "There was a huge disaster and I couldn't break away. Thank you for taking my briefcase." His voice would drop low, his words caressing away my anger. "I should have told you what was happening. You have every right to be upset with me. Let's give this another try tonight, somewhere quiet and romantic." His hand would cover mine. "I just want to get to know you."

"I want to get to know you too," I murmured.

"Pardon me?"

What?

The man at the table to my right was looking at me with eyebrows raised. Omigod, had I just said that out loud?

I let out a shaky laugh. "Just thinking through a philosophical problem for my job as a...philosopher." I rubbed a finger across my lips thoughtfully. "Why are people attracted to other people? What makes one person want to get to know someone else?"

The man stared at me, his smile frozen. Why, oh why,

couldn't I keep my mouth shut? I stood. "If you'll excuse me..." I strolled to the buffet counter and got a custard-filled, chocolate frosted donut. And a second one. If I was going to be stuck at continental breakfast for hours, I might as well enjoy it. Then I opened the USA Today and read every section. Twice. I'd never been so up-to-date on current events in my life.

After a couple of hours eating more than I needed, drinking enough coffee to give me the jitters, and no sign of Colin, I headed to work still in possession of the brief-case. Seemed pointless to leave it at the hotel front desk when the staff didn't know who Colin was, and there was no guarantee he had a room there anymore.

I screeched into a parking space in the lot next to Flaw-less Paws, hauled the duffle holding my jeans and t-shirt from the back seat, and dashed down the alley into the back door of the shop. I'd cut it so close, I only had a few minutes before my first appointment arrived. As soon as the door closed behind me, I kicked off Jen's heels and changed clothes. With only seconds to spare, I raced to unlock the front door.

I knew it. Appointment number one was already outside waiting. I opened the door and the sleigh bells tied to the handle jingled merrily.

"Good morning Pearl! Good morning Ivory!" I said to

the white miniature poodles that pranced into the shop ahead of their glamorous, silver-haired owner, Lily. She was the epitome of that saying, *white is the new blond.* I had no doubt she got plenty of second looks. Especially when she and the dogs were out and about together, which I suspected was more the norm than not.

As I checked Pearl and Ivory in, other dogs began to arrive for early drop-off. I was glad to be thrust into my typical busy day, so I could forget all about both the briefcase and Colin.

A few hours later, as I was putting the finishing touches on a gray schnoodle, the bells on the front door jangled. A black and white pit bull with a head the size of a bowling ball came through the door, his coloring and build giving him the appearance of a mini Holstein cow. The guy holding his leash was wearing a Twins cap so low on his forehead I couldn't even see his eyes. But it was hard to miss the nice shadow of a beard on his strong jaw.

Definitely a new customer because I would never have forgotten this guy. Or his dog.

"Hi, I'm Allie. Can I help you?" I asked from the grooming station.

The two big dogs—a golden retriever and a standard poodle—that I was letting roam loose in the shop ran up to the counter to greet the new arrival. But since the counter created a wall between the lobby and grooming area, they had to be content with wagging their tails and sniffing the air.

"I don't have an appointment," the guy said. "But any chance you can squeeze my dog in for a bath?"

I was booked solid. But I hated to turn away new customers because plenty of days weren't as busy as today happened to be. "Give me a minute to put this guy in the back and I'll check."

After depositing the schnoodle in a kennel in the back room, I hustled out. "Welcome to Flawless Paws by the way."

"Sorry to stop in without an appointment." He pulled off his cap.

I met his gaze and was rendered momentarily speechless. Words flashed through my brain. Handsome, not pretty. *Rugged.* Sandy brown hair. And his eyes...blue. Cool blue. Piercing blue. Blue that looked like it held secrets and kissed really well.

The combination of that face and those eyes almost made me stop breathing. I gave myself a mental slap upside the head. "N-No problem," I stammered. "I love walk-ins. The thing is..." I scrolled through my schedule on the computer. There was a possibility I could squeeze him in during the afternoon, but otherwise my only choice was to stay late and bathe his dog last. "I'm pretty booked—"

"He rolled in something smelly in the woods. You know dogs..." He gave me an imploring look.

The realization that I held the key to removing the desperation in those cool blue eyes sent a zinger from my stomach to my nether parts. Oh my God, really? I was so desperate to find a man to impress my family, I'd become positively hopeless. I knew nothing about this guy and my insides still did a shimmy as we were talking.

I grinned. "I'll find a way to fit him in. Can you do a late pickup, say six-thirty?" My schedule was so tight, I had no business adding another dog. But I couldn't afford to turn away customers, and if he became a regular, today's stress would be worth it.

Besides, maybe I would eventually learn that he was a...hedge fund manager, a self-made man who ruled the financial world. My parents would *love* that. Maybe as he brought his dog in for appointments we'd get to know one another better and our relationship would become something more. *"Oh, hi,"* I would say when he and his dog arrived. *"It's great to see you again."* And he would reply, *"I really love coming in here and not just because of—"*

"Thanks. That'd be great. His name's Petey."

My mind snapped back to the present, my cheeks began to warm. Ohmigod, my face was betraying my thoughts? At least this guy had no idea the thoughts running though my head.

"Like the pit bull in The Little Rascals," I said smoothly.

"Most people don't get it." His pensive smile made me feel like I'd just been admitted to an exclusive club that had very few members.

"Has that same patch around his eye." I felt ridiculously happy that I was one of the people who got it—even though it was pure luck. My grandpa had been a boy when the original Little Rascals came out in the thirties, and he'd delighted in introducing me to them when Hollywood brought out a remake. I had to remember to thank him for keeping me current.

"I'll need your dog's particulars." I handed him a pen and customer intake form so he could provide details about Petey's breed, name, age, fears, likes, favorite treats, etc. As he filled out the form, I took a fistful of mini dog treats from a jar on the counter and gave one each to his dog, the golden retriever, and the standard poodle. The rest I shoved into the front pocket of my jeans to be doled out throughout the day.

"Treats come in handy, huh?" He pointed at the jar.

"Helps make them behave. They'll do practically anything for these yummies."

He slid the completed form across the counter, answers scrawled messily across the sheet.

"I usually let a few of the big dogs roam behind the counter if they're going to be here for a while." I gestured at the dogs standing beside me. "They're happier not cooped up all day. Are you open to that with Petey? How is he with other dogs?"

"He loves other dogs. I'm okay with it as long as they all play nice."

"Never had a problem yet. Knock on wood." I tapped my fist on the Formica countertop and immediately felt dumb. "Okay then—" I focused on the form he'd filled out and squinted at his name, almost illegibly written. "Mr. Kelly. Jack—"

"Jax," he said.

"Oh, like Jack, plural?"

He grimaced painfully, like he'd had this conversation a million times before. "Like Jacksonville International Airport. I was born there...four weeks early. My mom thought the airport code made a great name. J-A-X."

"Good thing you weren't born in Nantucket."

He raised his brows.

"It's A-C-K. Ack."

A sharp laugh burst out of him. "She thought Jax worked out so well, she did it on purpose with my brother, Auggie."

"Auggie? Too many letters."

"Augusta, Maine. A-U-G. When we were kids, he made me promise never to call him anything but Auggie."

"I guess I can understand why."

He flashed me a grin, and a feeling zizzed through me, that sensation you get in your stomach when your car barrels too fast over the top of a hill and goes a bit airborne and you become weightless for a few seconds.

My cheeks started to burn again, and I quickly bent

over the counter to talk to Petey and hide my face—even though, truth be told, all I really wanted to do was stare at Jax Kelly. "Okay, pup, you get a play day today," I chirped. "Come on back and meet some new friends." I unhooked the hinged counter and flipped it up, then unlatched the Dutch half door beneath and swung it open to let Petey inside.

Once it was obvious that he and the other two dogs were going to get along great, I turned to Jax, determined to keep myself from viscerally reacting to his good looks and natural charm. "Okay, then, late pickup at six-thirty."

"Great." He shot me a lopsided grin, and my defenses crumbled under an onslaught of zizz.

Obviously I was a failure at visceral control.

Petey nuzzled his nose against my pocket where the treats were stashed. Jax watched the dog for a long moment. "Better be careful," he said as he headed outside. "Now that he knows where the treats are, he'll be begging all day."

"Don't worry," I said with a grin. "I've got in all in control."

I should have known better than to tempt fate.

FIVE

By noon, I'd had text message check-ins from both Megan and Bree—but no call from Colin. In the middle of grooming a geriatric schnauzer who kept dozing off on the table, my phone vibrated in my pocket. One hand firmly on the dog, I tugged out the phone, hoping it would be Colin, only to see my mother's number on the screen. I hesitated, then swiped it on, knowing that if I didn't answer, she'd not only leave a message, but would keep calling until she reached me.

"Jen told me all your exciting news," she said cheerily.

Oh, good. At least the gossip mill was alive and well. And what had I expected anyway? The lies I told Jen were just the kind of news my mother loved. I let out an audible sigh and tamped down the urge to make an excuse to get off the phone. Since I'd have to talk to her sooner or later, it might as well be sooner. At least I could cut the call short saying I had dogs to groom.

"Yeah, I met a guy, a friend of a friend. He's just in town for a few days, but he seems really nice." I told her about Colin, even though the only visage in my mind at that moment belonged to Jax. I described Colin's features, his eyes, his hair, his job...and took great satisfaction in the fact that my mother seemed duly impressed.

"Honey, he sounds wonderful. I hope we get a chance to meet him. And the dean?" Mom asked. "Jen said you were meeting with the dean about vet school."

Why had I even mentioned stupid vet school to Jen? Maintaining an out-and-out lie about vet school was going to a lot harder than keeping up a little white lie about Colin.

"Ohhh, it went okay," I said slowly. "But there's more to getting in than just applying. There are a bunch of steps and nothing is for sure." I didn't even know if that was true, but hoped it would stop her from assuming I'd be accepted and enrolled in vet school by next semester.

After blathering a few more possibly untrue statements about vet school entrance, I changed the topic back to Colin and began to talk nonstop so she couldn't get a word in edgewise. "Colin is so awesome, I really think you'd like him and so would Dad. There's just something about him that is so professional, so...together, and really, I mean, what he has to offer is so—"

"Honey," Mom interjected. "Listen, your dad could put in a good word with—"

"Oh, Mom, but Colin—"

"Your Dad knows the Dean, he can—"

Aaaahhhh. My stomach began to churn. If Dad talked to the dean he'd learn I was lying in five seconds flat. "No. Mom. No. Too soon. I haven't made up my mind yet so let's not get carried away. I really have to go. I've got a dog up on the table and he's getting antsy." Lie, lie, lie, lie, lie. That old schnauzer was practically asleep. "I'll call you later."

I tried to breathe like I'd learned in the meditation class the Megan, Bree, and I had taken. In in in through my nose, then out out out through my mouth. Inhaale. Exhaale. Inhaaaaale. Exhaaaaale. Gradually, my pulse dropped to normal and my stomach unclenched. I loved my parents, but why did they make me feel so inadequate?

By mid-afternoon, just as I was beginning to genuinely despair about hearing from Colin, Bree bounced through the door with a greasy high school kid in tow—skinny, black t-shirt, longish hair in need of a shampoo. I couldn't wait to find out what this was about.

The door banged shut behind them, and the sleigh bells on the knob jangled as if a reindeer had pranced into the room.

"This is Phinneas," Bree said.

"Finn," he said as he pulled up his saggy jeans.

The small mixed breed that I was grooming like a foo-foo poodle began to wiggle, excited that new people were in the shop. I shut off the clipper and carried him over to the counter so I could let Bree and Finn through the Dutch door. The three big dogs ran forward to greet them, and Finn took a cautious step back.

"Don't worry—they're all friendly," I said. "They're just getting some time off for good behavior."

"Cool." Finn reached a tentative hand down to rub the top of Petey's head. The dog's mouth opened in a shark-sized grin; his big tongue dangled out, dripping saliva onto the floor and Finn's shoe. *Nice.*

"So, what's up?" I asked.

"Phinneas can get into your briefcase," Bree said.

"Finn," the kid said again.

Bree ignored him. "You know, the briefcase that's locked...the one you lost the keys to. *The one you can't get open?*" Bree fixed her eyes on mine.

Obviously she'd spun a tale to this kid and wanted me to go along with it. I tried to decipher exactly what she was saying—that Finn could literally *break into* the case? I looked from one to the other. "You mean like, break the locks?" I put the dog back on the grooming table and hooked him up to the harness.

"That sounds so...harsh," Bree said as Finn inspected his fingernails. "*Pick the locks* is more the phrasing I would use."

"Seriously?" I glanced over at Finn. He seemed utterly engrossed in cleaning out his nails. "Is that really something I want to do?"

"Do you want to get your important paperwork out of it or not?" Bree countered.

I quietly hissed out a breath. Without a doubt, Colin's contact information was in that briefcase. If we could just get inside it, all we had to do was find a phone number and lock the case back up. No harm, no foul. He would never have to know. "Well, yeah," I said slowly. "How about...Megan?"

"She doesn't know how to pick locks."

Oh, great. Bree hadn't run this by Megan. We were contemplating taking an action that was probably illegal without getting any legal guidance.

I unobtrusively scrutinized Finn. He was clean-shaven —probably because he was too young to actually grow much facial hair. Maybe he was older than he appeared, but I doubted it. Just a kid. Based on the typical teenage attention span, he'd forget all about this in ten minutes. Maybe five. "I don't want to wreck the locks," I said to Bree. "Can he do it without wrecking the locks?"

Finn nodded.

"He's been suspended twice already for picking locks at school. It would have been three times but I, ah, ah—"

"She lied for me."

"The third time would have meant expulsion," Bree said, coloring. "He's got so much potential, you see..."

Ohmyfreakinggod. Bree tended to see the world in black and white. And here she was dancing in gray city. I was speechless.

"Where's the briefcase?" the kid asked.

"How old are you?"

"Fifteen."

Fifteen. Reality began to rear its ugly head. Underage. Breaking and entering.

If taking stuff out of people's garbage cans was considered theft, surely breaking into a locked briefcase was something equally bad. Ugh.

Well, I rationalized, if this was against the law, which I was pretty sure it was, Bree and I might go to jail for contributing to the delinquency of a minor, but at least he would only be going to juvie. Somehow the thought didn't cheer me. The dog began fidgeting on the table, pulling against the harness holding him in place. "Let me quick finish this guy and I'll get the briefcase," I said.

Five minutes later, I had retrieved the case from my car and set it on the desk in the back room.

"Dual combination locks." Finn's voice cracked, reminding me how young he was. "Left and right could be different combinations." He pulled a paperclip from his pocket and straightened it.

I rolled my eyes. Surely, the CEO of the Intercontinental Jewelry Exchange would not have a briefcase that could be breached with a paperclip. Finn stuck the end of the paperclip into the lock and began to gently wiggle it around. A minute passed and another and then a couple more.

"Listen," I said, "this is a high-end attaché. I don't think a paperclip will—"

Finn snapped open the first lock and went to work on the second.

I raised impressed brows at Bree.

"You should see him on a computer," she said.

"He needs to put these skills to work for the good." I turned to Finn. "You need to put these skills to work for the good, Finn. Stay in the light. The sunshine needs people like you."

"Why do you think I lied for him?" Bree said. "I wanted him to have a chance to learn about the positive opportunities for using his amazing abilities."

"Like breaking into briefcases?" Finn asked.

I snorted out a laugh. I liked this kid. "*Besides* breaking into briefcases. If you're as smart as Bree says, people will be knocking down your door. You can make big money someday."

The kid popped open the second lock, then gave a quick grin. "Speaking of money..." he said to Bree.

"Oh yeah." She picked a piece of lint off her sleeve. "I said you'd give him twenty bucks."

"No problem." I pulled twenty dollars from the till and handed it to him. "Thank you very much. I can't tell you how happy you've made me."

Finn pointed at the back door that led to the alley. "Can I get out that way?"

"Don't you need a ride, Phinneas?" Bree asked.

He shook his head. "Going over to Ben's."

"Okay, well thanks for coming. See you tomorrow." Bree waved.

"Yuh," he grunted in reply. The door crashed shut behind him, and neither of us moved for a few seconds.

"Why do you insist on calling him Phinneas?" I asked.

"It's his name. And it means oracle. You know, like the mystics who foretell the future," Bree explained. "He's such a special kid, and I just want him to realize that, you know? That *he* can be the future. That he actually *has* a future." She sighed. "That is, if he quits breaking the law."

"And today really helped reinforce that *not breaking the law thing.*" I flipped open the attaché. "Okay, let's get this over with. Every minute this case is open, I feel guilty."

The contents of Colin's briefcase looked like he'd come straight from the office supply store. I flipped through several pads of practically new yellow legal paper and a number of empty manila folders.

Bree reached into a pocket and withdrew a small cloth bag with a zipper top. "Oh, don't tell me, don't tell me what's in here," she said in a hushed voice. She opened the zipper and gasped, then held the bag open for me to see. Jewelry sparkled inside—necklaces and bracelets studded with diamonds, sapphires, emeralds, and more diamonds. "I don't think we're in Kansas anymore," she said.

"No. And we're not going to be in this briefcase much longer either. Zip that bag." I began to rifle through the rest of the stuff in the briefcase. There wasn't a business card or piece of company stationary in sight. And not a word had been written on anything. "This screams *first day on a new job*. When you don't even know what you're supposed to do yet. How can there not be a business card in here?"

"Maybe because he has a wallet," Bree said. "That's probably where his business cards are." She opened another cloth bag and let out a low whistle. "Wow, more of the same. Colin has to be going crazy thinking this stuff is lost."

"*I'm* going crazy thinking this stuff is lost. I can't believe he hasn't tried to reach me." I held up a small, padded yellow envelope and gave it a shake. It didn't make a sound.

"Open it." Bree swirled a finger. "Maybe there's a receipt inside, or a sheet with contact information."

"What if it's something private—?"

"Something he'll never see again if we can't find him."

I tapped the edge of the envelope lightly on the fingers of my other hand. "I don't want Colin to think I'm a snoop."

"If he doesn't understand you opened it to try to help him, well, then who wants him?"

She made a good point. "Yeah, okay." I pried open the flap with a letter opener, then reached into the envelope to pull out a lumpy, oddly folded sheet of paper. Slowly, I peeled back each of the folds to reveal a diamond ring with a big, oval stone. Big like a Brussel sprout. Okay, big like a small Brussel sprout. Easily half an inch. Bigger than any diamond I had ever seen except on TV.

"My God," Bree breathed. "That's no receipt. Do you think it's real?"

I cupped the ring in my palm and gaped at it in awe. "I doubt the Intercontinental Jewelry Exchange does much business in cubic zirconias."

"That diamond has so many carats it's almost a turnip."

Brussel sprouts. Turnips. There was a theme here. "What does that mean?"

"You know Richard Burton, that old movie star? He said it about some diamond he gave Elizabeth Taylor. It just seemed appropriate at the moment."

I gave my head a shake as if to clear my thoughts. "This stuff has to be worth hundreds of thousands of dollars. How does someone leave behind a briefcase this valuable? And why isn't he moving heaven and earth to find it?"

"Maybe he wanted you to have it." Bree gave a little shimmy.

"Ahhh, that must be it. Meet a woman at breakfast, give her a life supply of gems over drinks, including a diamond ring big enough for a royal wedding." I walked through the doorway into the front room of the shop and held the diamond up to shimmer gloriously in the beams of afternoon sunlight striping the room. I grinned over my shoulder at Bree. "Maybe it's an engagement present."

The bells at the front door jangled as a middle-aged

woman came into the shop. I closed my fingers around the gem and shoved it into the front pocket of my jeans.

"I'm here for Jasper," she said as the three big dogs hustled over to the counter.

I went into rote check-out mode: retrieve the dog from its kennel, give it a treat from the jar on the counter, get payment, schedule the next appointment, say goodbye to both dog and owner, and then send them on their way with a merry, "Thank you! See you next time!"

As soon as they were out the door, I hurried into the back room where Bree was meticulously combing through the briefcase again. "Anything?" I asked.

She made a face that clearly meant *no.*

"What type of person would keep all this jewelry in a briefcase with no identification?"

"Cat burglars. Mafia. Thieves. Murderers." Bree frowned. "Maybe you're in way over your head."

My breath caught. "You're scaring me. You don't really think that, do you?"

"Well, no. He's probably just a regular guy who happens to be in the gem business. But I'd feel a lot better if there was some identification."

"Yeah." I worried my lower lip. "Probably doesn't keep I.D. in there so if he gets robbed, the jewel thieves can't track him down and show up demanding more stuff."

"Yeahhhh. Or else he's a cat burglar or mafia or—"

"Or we've been watching too many movies. I'm as nervous as you are. But I don't think it's fair to think the worst of Colin yet. Let's put everything back the way we found it. Tonight, I'll scour the Internet for information about the Intercontinental Jewelry Exchange." I pointed at her. "Since you're done with work, why don't you call some other jewelry organizations to see if they have contact info for Colin or the Exchange?"

"What if we don't find anything? Aren't you a little nervous having all this jewelry in your possession?"

I exhaled. Twenty-four hours ago we were all practically convinced Colin was *the one who was meant to be.* And now... "I think we have to give him another day and then, if there's no word...we call the police? Deal?"

Bree smoothed flat the small square paper the diamond ring had been folded inside. "Deal."

I reached into my pocket and rooted around for the ring, finally pulling the thing out in a fistful of mini dog treats. The three big dogs crowded against me begging for a yummy.

"No!" I said firmly. I took a step back and held out my open palm to Bree, the diamond ring sparkling like a treasure among the treats.

"That's one pretty little Cracker Jack prize." Bree reached for the ring just as Petey rammed his nose upward against the bottom of my hand. The handful of treats went flying along with the ring, and Bree and I screamed like kids at a birthday party when the piñata bursts open.

The dogs went crazy, tails whipping like windmills as they gobbled up everything as soon as it landed on the old hardwood floor. I corralled two of the mongrels by the collar, Bree grabbed the third, and we shoved them into lower kennels and latched the doors.

"Did you see where it went?" Bree was breathing hard like she'd just finished a marathon.

I shook my head furiously. We dropped to hands and knees and began to crawl around, searching. "It has to be here," I said. "It has to be." We couldn't have—*we just couldn't* have lost that ring.

We spent nearly half an hour hunting through the back room, both of us refusing to say out loud what appeared to be our new reality—every last one of the treats was gone. And so was the ring.

I sat back on my heels and let my gaze slide over the room while my thoughts skittered every which way. "This can't be happening. I refuse to accept this."

Bree seemed to be in shock. She waved her hands. "It must be here somewhere. A diamond ring can't just disappear. Especially one with so many carats it's almost a turnip."

"It's not that big," I said testily. I looked at the three dogs on their feet at the front of their cages, wagging, wagging, wagging, mouths open, panting, panting, wagging, wagging—

Oh no. My breath started to come in shallow bursts. "It didn't disappear." I started to hyperventilate and cupped my hands over my mouth. "Oh. My. God. Bree. It's with the dog treats. Inside one of those dogs. They ate it."

"That's ridiculous. Diamonds don't have a flavor."

"Clearly you've never had a dog," I said through my cupped hands. "Stuff doesn't need to taste good for dogs to eat it. Gloves, socks, stones...our old basset hound used to eat marbles."

Bree closed her eyes a moment. "And then what?"

"What do you think?" I said, my tone now waspish. "Sparkliest poop in town."

We stared at the dogs. I felt like getting sick.

"Well. Guess I have to get going." Bree pushed herself to standing, straightened her skirt, and dusted off her bare knees. "Let me know how everything works out, okay?" After a long beat, the corners of her mouth curved up. "Just kidding."

I began to chuckle and she joined in, and we laughed until we were guffawing, until we were gasping for air and I had started to cry at the same time. "How does this stuff happen to me? I meet a handsome guy with a great personality and an awesome job. Then he disappears without a word and the next thing you know, his diamond ring has been eaten by one of my client's dogs and I'm talking about sparkly poop. Is it any wonder my family thinks I'm a screw-up? I *am* a screw-up."

Tears cascaded over my cheeks as I alternated between sobbing and laughing. Bree patted me on the shoulder. "It's not your fault—it's my fault. If I hadn't brought Phinneas over, we would never have gotten into the briefcase. Blame me. It's my fault."

"Well, following that line of thinking…" I drew a shuddering breath. "If we'd never gone to continental breakfast, we wouldn't have had a briefcase to break into in the first place. So, it's Megan's fault."

"Works for me." Bree studied the three big dogs. "You troublemakers are going to be behind bars for a while. So how long will it take for it to…?"

"Come into the light? I don't know. I never paid attention with the marbles."

Bree went to the front of the shop to retrieve her phone from her purse, then ran a Google search. "According to the Internet gods, one or two days." She tapped the screen some more. "Yeah, that should do it. Not so bad, is it?" she said with exaggerated optimism.

"Three dogs, three different owners," I said. "It's bad."

"How are you going to tell them?" Bree stuck her fingers through the wire front of a top row cage to pet one of the smaller dogs.

I scooped up the diamond folding paper from where it had fluttered to the floor and threw it into the briefcase, then stuck the case high on a shelf without latching the locks. "I have no idea. What can I say that doesn't sound absurd? I mean, come on—an international gem company, a big diamond ring, three hungry dogs…"

I gestured at the clock on the wall and let out a whimper. "It's nearly four, and now I'm really behind. I'm booked solid today, even squeezed in a walk-in." I couldn't bring myself to admit to Bree that I took the walk-in because his owner was amazingly good-looking and had unbelievable eyes. "And the thanks I got for taking that walk-in? Well, guess which dog hit my hand and caused this whole mess. Not complaining because I need the business, but still."

I carried a small scraggily mixed breed over to the tub for a bath. Bree stood beside me as I lathered him up.

"Maybe you could promise those three owners free dog grooming for a year if they bring in all their...*do-do*." She distastefully scrunched up her nose.

"That's assuming I can trust whoever finds the ring will actually give it to me." I sudsed the dog's legs. "It's anyone's guess what people will do when confronted with a get rich quick card...especially one that has so many carats it's almost a turnip. What the hell does that even mean anyway?"

"You know, carats...as in how diamonds are weighed? And then carrots, those crunchy, orange things that you eat?" Bree said as though that explained everything.

"And what do carrots that you eat have to do with turnips, other than both are root vegetables?" I asked grumpily.

Bree shrugged, and I let out a snort.

"I think there's only one thing to do," I said. "I have to keep all three dogs overnight." I twisted the sprayer knob until the water was warm, and began to rinse the dog in the tub. "Two are regular customers. With a good enough excuse, I'm sure I can convince their owners to leave them.

But that pit bull's brand new—I don't know anything about his owner except what he told me this morning."

"So, just make the reason ironclad. What would make people agree to leave their pets overnight? What would make them *want to* leave them?"

"Exposure to disease would probably do it. Maybe kennel cough, it's really contagious—"

The bells on the front door jangled and a beefy middle-aged man stepped into the shop. He definitely hadn't dropped off a dog today, but that didn't mean he wasn't picking one up. *Please, please, please*, I silently begged the universe, *let him be selling ad space in some publication and not here to pick up one of the ring swallowers.*

"Be right with you," I called.

I left Bree to watch the dog I'd just bathed, and decided if the man was here for one of the infamous three, I would use the kennel cough lie to keep him from taking the dog. Weak, I knew, but the best I had at that moment.

As I reached the counter, he smiled broadly. "I'm Tom Davis," he said as though I would recognize his name.

"Are you here to pick up a dog?"

"No. I work with Colin Hughes. We got the message you left at the hotel."

SIX

I FELT THE BLOOD DRAIN FROM MY FACE, MAYBE EVEN FROM MY whole body. All at once, I was chilled. My hands were white and shaking. My brain was non-functioning, like a computer with a crashed hard drive, the last file in its memory frozen on the screen. For me, that file was a picture of the diamond ring.

"Oh," I managed to squeak out. "Is Colin okay?"

A line formed between Davis's brows. "Fine. He's fine."

"Was it bad news? Did he have to go to Zurich?"

Davis pressed his lips together, and I knew I had overstepped. This was private company business, and Colin had probably told me more than he should have last night.

"Yes, it was. One of our other...there was an accident. Colin left...for Zurich."

With that, my brain unlocked and one word rose to prominence: *filibuster.* Tom Davis was obviously here for the briefcase, but if I could prevent him from asking for it, I would never have to admit I'd broken into it and lost the ring.

Yes, I realized this took me to a level of insanity, but all I could think was: desperate times call for desperate measures. So I started to talk. Ramble might be a better word. "Have you seen how nice this dog grooming shop is? And what a cute name—*Flawless Paws*. I'm a rep for a dog food manufacturer. Have been doing an in-service here all day and this place is really one of the best—"

Davis tried to interrupt, but I waved him off.

"Many shops and veterinarians stock better brands of dog food as a service to their customers. That's why I'm here today, finding out how we can better serve the needs of dog groomers and, by extension, the needs of their customers and their dogs..."

As I blabbered on, it dawned on me that I was very quickly going to run out of things to say. I needed something much longer and more substantial if I were to carry the day. Suddenly my recitation from eighth grade forensics competition leapt to the forefront: *The Highwayman*. Perfect! Hopefully I still remembered it. I straightened my shoulders and dove in.

"The Highwayman by Alfred Noyes. The wind was a torrent of darkness among the gusty trees. The moon was a ghostly galleon tossed upon cloudy seas. The road was a ribbon of moonlight over the purple moor, and the highwayman came

riding—riding—riding— The highwayman came riding, up to the old inn-door."

I glanced over my shoulder at Bree. She was staring at me with round eyes and a half-smile. Tom Davis looked shell-shocked. He glanced over at Bree, too. "Excuse me," he said, "Excuse me, I just need to—"

"He'd a French cocked-hat on his forehead, a bunch of lace at his chin," I loudly said over him, gesturing melodramatically to indicate the highwayman's clothing. *"A coat of the claret velvet, and breeches of brown doe-skin. They fitted with never a wrinkle. His boots were up to the thigh. And he rode with a jeweled twinkle, His pistol butts a-twinkle, His rapier hilt a-twinkle, under the jeweled sky."*

I was getting dizzy from not breathing properly, so I paused for the teeniest second to suck in a big breath. "Over the cobbles he clattered and clashed in the dark inn-yard, He tapped with his whip on the shutters, but all was locked and barred—"

"I'm here to get Colin's briefcase," Davis shouted.

I froze, mouth open.

"But we haven't even gotten to the part about Bess, the landlord's black-eyed daughter," Bree cried, frantically nodding at me to continue.

I nodded back. "He whistled a tune to the window, and who should be waiting there, But the landlord's black-eyed daughter—"

"Stop!" Tom Davis growled. Really, he growled it like he might come roaring over the counter like a tiger. "I need Colin's briefcase. Now, do you still have it?"

Filibuster broken. I swallowed hard. I would never make it in politics. "Yes, of course."

"Bess, the landlord's daughter, plaiting a dark red love-knot into her long black hair," Bree whispered.

"It's in the back room," I said. "I'll get it for you." My legs felt like wooden four-by-fours, my knees stiff and unbending as I walked toward the back room.

Bree looked as unnerved as I was. She hastily wrapped the wet dog in a towel and charged past me, all the while, murmuring inanities to make it appear that she actually was a dog groomer. "Okay, sweet poochie poo, you just need to air dry for a bit, then we'll comb you out and you'll be so pretty for your mama."

She deposited the dog in a cage, then whirled round. "What do we do?" she whispered, flapping her arms like she was trying to get airborne.

"I don't know." I caught sight of the back exit, and for one irrational moment considered running. "What do *you* think we should do?"

"Lock the briefcase, give it to him, and keep our mouths shut."

"Maybe I should tell the truth and beg for mercy."

"And have him call the police to lock us up for theft?" Bree held up both hands like she was surrendering. "At least this will buy us some time. As long as Colin's in Zurich, he won't be opening the briefcase. By the time he's back, we'll have recovered the diamond and you can return it. No worries."

No worries seemed like a bit of an understatement. "If I don't own up to it ahead of time, he's going to think I tried to steal it." I lifted the briefcase off the shelf and set it on the desk.

Bree shook her head. "No, you're wrong. If you give him the diamond as soon as he's back and immediately explain what happened, it'll all be fine. He'll probably laugh. I'll back up your story—I was here. If we have to, we can even have him talk to the owners of the three dogs. That should be plenty of proof you're telling the truth."

"It's a huge risk." I refolded the diamond paper and slid it into the padded envelope, then pressed the flap down so the adhesive stuck. I pictured myself seeing Colin again, gazing into his eyes and saying, *"I didn't intend to steal anything. I was just trying to get your briefcase back to you. No harm, no foul."* He would smile and say, *"I understand,"* as he took my hands in his. Then he would lean in to kiss me and whisper: *"Liar!"* His hands would tighten around my wrists. *"You lied about being a dog food sales rep, you lied about where you lived. I know you took the diam—"*

"Allie?"

I blinked hard. "I guess your option is better than the alternative." I snapped both latches shut and spun the numbers on the dual combination locks. What choice did I have? It sure didn't make sense to tell a complete stranger that I broke into his colleague's briefcase and then, somehow, lost a diamond ring—oh, excuse me, let a dog swallow it. The story was so ludicrous, I would be in jail before dinner. Or maybe hauled in for a mental evaluation once he told the police how I'd charged into a recitation of *The Highwayman*.

"I sure hope we're right." Clasping the briefcase to my chest, I plastered on a smile and went out to the counter. "Here it is," I chirped, handing it over.

Tom Davis wiped a fist across his forehead in mock relief. "Thanks. It would have been quite a blow to lose... what's inside here." He patted the briefcase and started for the door.

"You're a liar." Colin whispered in my mind. "Everything's a lie. Your job, your business trip, losing the diamond..."

I couldn't do this. It was wrong in so many ways. Besides, with my history of luck, it would all blow up somehow. Much as Bree wanted to believe otherwise, it was never going to be *no worries*.

"Uhhh, can you tell Colin I say *hi* and that, um, I'd love to hear about Zurich and, honestly, there is just one thing I need you to tell him for me..."

"Allie, we have so much to get done today," Bree interrupted, "why don't you just talk to Colin when he's back?"

"But—"

"I mean it. We're already behind," Bree said in her take-charge teacher's voice.

Somehow, I felt like we were living that proverb—*when you find yourself in a hole, stop digging.* Maybe the problem was we hadn't dug deep enough yet. Maybe we had to be in over our heads and that's when we'd know it was time to come clean.

I dipped my chin at Bree, then turned to Tom Davis. "Just tell him I said, *hi.*"

Bree and I were so stunned by what had just transpired—that we'd handed over the briefcase without the ring—we didn't speak for the next five minutes. I kept doing my work, and she silently followed me around the shop like a magnet.

"At least we don't have to worry about losing any more gems," she finally said.

"Great. All we have to worry about is *finding one.*"

We fell into morose silence until Megan texted us about meeting up later that night for Friday Happy Hour. It sounded like the perfect end to a stressful week—half-price drinks and free appetizers. "Unfortunately, I'll be on poop patrol," I said wistfully. "Which...I must admit sounds infinitely more interesting than drinking beer and eating Buffalo wings and potato skins. I think it'll be lots more fun to play with the dogs and—"

"Nice try."

I sighed. "You guys have a good time."

Bree patted my arm, then pushed through the door. "Text us after you talk with the dog owners. We'll stop by later with a bottle of wine."

After Bree was gone, I went into overdrive, bathing and clipping dogs as fast as I could. In between, I also called the owners of the golden retriever and the standard poodle and told each of them...a slight falsehood. Since I'd always heard that the most believable lies are those closest to the truth, I said I'd dropped my ring when I took it off to wash my hands, and their dog had gobbled it up thinking it was a treat. Both owners were appropriately appalled and apologetic, and each agreed to let me keep their dog overnight—or until I got the ring back.

It helped that I'd been grooming the two dogs for a few years, so the owners knew and trusted me. Jax Kelly, on the other hand, didn't know me at all, and I had a sneaking suspicion he wasn't going to readily agree to my plan. Which is why I'd put off calling him until last.

As I put the finishing touches on a sweet little terrier, it dawned on me there was more than one way to skin a cat. What about X-rays? How could Bree and I not have thought of this before? Obviously, the stress of the last twenty-four hours had affected our problem-solving abilities, shut down our cerebrums or something. I pulled out my phone. All I had to do was have each dog scanned, and I could instantly narrow the field from three to one.

I pulled up the phone number of a nearby vet, then let out a groan. It was Friday; nobody had extended hours on Friday night. By the time all my customers picked up their dogs, only the emergency vet clinic would still be open— and Flawless Paws wasn't so successful I could afford to pay their premium, after-hours prices. Especially not for three sets of X-rays.

"Story of my life. Great idea, too late." Discouraged, I went to the front counter to retrieve Jax's contact information and punch his number into my phone. I tried to convince myself that everything would be fine, that I was just being too pessimistic. Maybe the connection we seemed to have this morning would be enough to convince him to trust me with Petey overnight. Although, to be honest, I wasn't exactly sure if we had a two-way thing or if it was just all me.

As soon as Jax picked up, I dove right into my story, explaining how I'd dropped my ring and Petey had eaten it.

"What?" He didn't sound pleased.

I gave a nervous chuckle. "He thought it was a treat. Not to worry, though," I said, feeling a prickling under my arms. "I spoke to the vet and he says it should safely pass in a day or two. But someone will have to look for it...if you know what I mean. So if it's all right with you, I'll spare you that job. I can keep him overnight and take care of all the, ah, monitoring."

There was such a long pause I thought our connection had dropped. But then I heard a car horn blaring and tires squealing. "Are you all right?"

"Yeah. Someone just made an illegal U-turn."

From the sounds of the background noise, I wondered if that someone was him.

"So, then, it's okay? I'll keep Petey overnight?"

"I don't think that'll work. He gets separation anxiety."

"I won't leave him alone," I said in my most reassuring voice. "I'm sure he'll be fine."

"I don't want to leave him in a cage overnight."

Part of me was touched by how much he loved his dog. And the rest of me was experiencing a surge of anxiety. I went into the back room to kneel next to Petey's kennel and began talking again, fast. "I'd never leave him in a cage. I'm planning to take him to my house overnight. He'll have treats and hugs and... I'll take him for a walk. Everything a dog could want. A Dalmatian vacation! Even though he's not actually a Dalmatian, just has the same black and white coloring," I said, cringing at my words. "And truly, as soon as I get my ring back—it belonged to my dear departed grandmother, did I mention that?—I'll call and you can pick him up—or I can drop him off, whatever is most convenient. Even if it's the middle of the night." I paused to grab a breath.

"Thanks, but I think it'll be easier if I take him home and do the monitoring myself."

This couldn't be happening. A million thoughts dashed through my brain at once and quickly spilled out over my lips. "Well, it's more than the ring actually. I cut his nails too close to the quick, so I ran him over to the vet to have them checked. And while he was there, he got exposed to kennel cough. Now the vet is insisting that he be quarantined for a day. So between my grandmother's ring and his exposure, well you can see how complicated the problem has become. I'm just so sorry and... I'd like to offer you free grooming for the rest of the year to make up for all this trouble."

A long pause followed. Long. Pause. Long enough for me to send up a desperate plea for help to every one of my deceased relatives.

Just when I was sure Jax must be about to cave, he said, "Why don't I come over there." Then he shut off the phone. Just like that, shut it off. No *goodbye*. No *thanks for squeezing in my dog today*. No *it was sure nice trading smiles with you this morning*. Nothing.

I huffed out a breath. So much for relying on divine intervention from dead family members.

I knew I couldn't wait any longer to make an appointment for X-rays—the clinic down the block was about to close for the day. So I decided to move forward on the assumption that I'd be able to convince Jax to leave Petey overnight. One way or another, by tomorrow morning I wanted to know which dog was the culprit.

As five o'clock came and went, pet owners also came and went picking up their dogs. Finally, only the three troublemakers were left, all still in the kennels where Bree and I had deposited them after the great diamond debacle.

I glanced at my watch. What happened to Jax? He'd sounded like he was coming right over, but more than an hour had passed since our call. I went into the back room to get the broom and waggled a finger at the guilty canines.

"Are you three happy with yourselves? Were those treats worth the trouble we're in? Because, to tell you the truth, they're making me feel sick and I didn't even eat any."

I stopped in front of Petey's cage. "As for you, well, that's the thanks I get for taking on a last minute customer? Apparently it's true—no good deed goes unpunished."

Petey's ears pricked up.

"I can't risk losing that diamond," I said. "You have to stay with me tonight. When your dad arrives, make no mistake about it, I will prevail."

By that point, all three dogs had come to the front of their kennels in anticipation of being set free. My anger waned. They had no idea they'd done anything wrong. To them, all my admonishments were nothing more than just a series of sounds. I let out a long sigh. "Oh, fine. You're forgiven. But you still can't come out until I finish sweeping up."

The sleigh bells jangled on the front door and my stomach took an excited flop. *Jax, finally.* It felt like one of the most important moments of my life. "Showtime," I whispered to the dogs. I set my shoulders, put on my warmest smile, and went out to convince Jax that leaving Petey overnight was the best option for us all.

Except the man who came through the door wasn't Jax; it was the guy who'd come in earlier, Colin's business associate, Tom Davis. And he didn't look nearly as friendly anymore either. A chill raced through me. He couldn't possibly know the diamond was missing, could he?

Maybe he just wanted to hear the rest of *The Highwayman*.

"You're back," I said in a chipper voice, though I felt anything but.

Tom Davis didn't return my smile.

"Hi again. Is there something else?" I wished Bree hadn't gone home.

"A piece is missing from Colin's briefcase."

The contents of my stomach tried to rise into my throat. I swallowed hard. The room began to buzz.

"I can explain," I croaked. I cleared my throat and repeated more forcefully, "I can explain." I forced a casual grin in an attempt to make a friendly connection. "When I didn't hear back from Colin, I had a—locksmith—open the case so I could get Colin's business card or phone number. I just wanted to tell him where he could pick up the briefcase." I sped up. "I wasn't trying to steal anything —I just wanted to find a way to reach Colin."

Tom Davis stared at me for too long, then finally said, "An extremely valuable item is gone." He rubbed his fore-head and, for the first time, I noticed all the fat gold rings on his left hand, kind of like brass knuckles. "As long as you return that item, we won't involve the police."

Police? I couldn't imagine their response to my story now, not with the latest twist. No one would believe it. I could hardly believe it myself and I knew it was true. Jail. I'd go to jail. *Do time.* I drew a slow breath and tried to talk myself down from the mountain peak of panic upon which

I was perched. "I would love to give it back—and I will. Soon. But I can't quite yet."

His eyes narrowed.

"What I mean is, I'll give it back as soon as I get it. But—"

"Where is it?"

Long fingers of fear wrapped around my belly.

"Who has it?" His voice dropped a notch

"I do. Don't worry. I have it." I gestured helplessly with one hand. "It's just not...readily accessible." In the most upbeat voice I could muster, I quickly explained what happened. "So you see, in another day, or two at the most, we should have the ring back. No harm, no foul. Then I'll just turn it over to you."

His scowl deepened. "You expect me to believe this?"

"Could anyone really make it up?"

He set a hand on the counter, and I instantly regretted my flippant reply.

"We—Colin and I don't have time to wait—that ring is in the process of being sold."

Of course it was. Nothing was ever simple, not in my life anyway. "I'm so sorry. You can't even imagine how sorry I am. If you could just explain to the buyer—"

"This could get dangerous."

"Pardon me?" My pulse began to throb in my ears.

"For the dog. It could perforate his intestine."

Was he really talking about the dog? Or was he implying something else? "I talked to the vet—"

"Where is the dog?"

"Pardon me?"

"Where. Is. The. Dog?" His voice, even lower than it was before, had taken on a frightening intensity.

I hesitated, trying to decide whether to tell him everything or not. With sudden clarity, I realized I had no choice. "He's in the back. But the problem is actually bigger than one dog." I winced. "Three dogs were loose. I'm not sure which one actually is the guilty party, so I'm monitoring all three."

"Three?" He tilted his head back and looked up at the ceiling as though contemplating his next action. Then he rubbed his forehead again with the hand adorned with gold rings, leveled his gaze on me and said, "Get them."

SEVEN

"WELL, IT'S NOT THAT SIMPLE," I SAID, MY VOICE RISING. "Whichever dog swallowed it will have to, uh, pass the diamond, so then someone will have to inspect each dog's...you know...to see..." A hysterical laugh escaped me and I cut it off. "It'll be messy business, if you get what I'm trying to say. That's why I'll just watch them and once the diamond gets passed—"

"There are faster ways to get a diamond out of a dog."

I forced myself not to react to his words. What faster ways? Was this guy threatening the dogs? Over my dead body would anything happen to them. "Mr. Davis, I assure you, we'll have the diamond before another day or two—"

"Get me the damn dogs." He pointed his index finger at me like a gun.

My heart skipped about four beats. Time screeched to

a halt and all the energy in the room buzzed like super-charged high tension electric wires. I held up a placating hand to buy some time. "Let me just leash them up," I said in the friendliest voice I could muster, at least three octaves higher than normal.

Once in the back room, I stopped in front the wall of kennels, all cages empty except for three on the bottom. The three dogs were on their feet and wagging their tails, trusting that my presence meant something good for them.

How had it come to this?

If it weren't for my job, I wouldn't be in this mess. My parents wouldn't be sighing with disappointment every time they saw me. I wouldn't be trying to meet a successful guy in the hopes that a romance would be enough to make Mom and Dad begin to take me seriously. And there wouldn't be a dangerous-looking man out in the lobby, pretending he was worried about the dogs, when the truth was, he probably had a gun jammed in the waistband of his pants under his jacket and all he really wanted was the diamond.

Maybe my parents were right; maybe I should have gone to vet school. I let out a sigh. The thing is, I like my job. Really, I do. I mean, there are parts of it that I don't love, like expressing anal glands, lalalalala, but everyone feels that way sometimes, don't they? Even the president has to hate his job once in a while and he has perks the rest of us can only dream of. On the other hand, the prez could probably totally relate to my problem with the guy in the lobby.

"Hurry up!" Tom Davis yelled, startling me into action.

"One minute," I called back. I opened the nearest kennel and hooked a leash to Petey's collar, making sure to rattle the cage door so Davis knew I was following through. Then I opened the kennels holding the golden retriever and the standard poodle and hooked them to leashes, too. The poodle pranced a bit, the pompoms that I had sculpted around his legs and tail seeming pretentious and absurd in the face of—

In the face of what? I couldn't even put words to what I was afraid Tom Davis had planned for these dogs. *There are faster ways to get a diamond out of a dog.* The blood pounded in my ears, my brain screamed for me to take action, but my feet stayed firmly rooted to the floor. The dogs were practically dancing, their tails fanning happy circles in anticipation of getting the usual *going home* treat. They had no clue that today's yummy might be the last one they ever got.

What should I do? I couldn't stay in the back room much longer. Sooner or later Tom Davis was going to come back there looking for me and the dogs. *And the diamond.*

Shit, shit, shit. This was all Megan's fault. If she'd never come up with the idea of going to continental breakfast in the first place, none of this would ever have happened.

"Hey," Tom Davis yelled.

I could hear him wiggling the counter and the Dutch

door, trying to open them so he could get to the other side. Wasn't going to work; both were latched underneath. If he wanted to get back here, he'd have to climb over. Which I didn't doubt he would do if I didn't hurry up.

"I'll be right out. Come on, pups," I practically shouted in my happy voice to make sure he heard. Whatever it was that Tom Davis wanted, we weren't sticking around to find out. I shoved one hand through the loop end of all three leashes and the other into my purse to find my car keys. Then I slung my purse over my head and across my chest, pushed open the alley door, and started to run.

All I needed was to get to my car. Get to my car and get inside. Get to my car and get inside and lock the doors. Get to my car and get inside and lock the doors and drive away. Four simple steps. The dogs and I were just a four-step, self-help program away from safety.

I bolted across the broken asphalt to the end of the alley, the three dogs bounding alongside like we were playing a game. Behind me, a door crashed against the wall, and I knew Tom Davis was hot on my heels. As the dogs and I sprinted out of the alley and across the parking lot, I made a quick calculation—if I stopped to open my car door and load in three dogs, Davis would catch us. I was better off running out to the sidewalk and into the street where there might be some traffic and other people.

Except it was Friday, dammit, and every nearby business had already closed for the day.

"Help!" I shrieked, hoping someone—anyone—was still around. "Help me!"

At the front of the lot, a man jumped out of his car and took a couple of steps in my direction. Tom Davis had an accomplice? I sucked in a breath and veered left to avoid getting anywhere near him.

The guy yelled, "Hey! Hey! Flawless Paws! Hey, that's my dog!"

I whipped my head back around. "Jax!" I screamed. Relief filled me. Relief and joy and zizz. I didn't think I'd ever been so happy to see anyone in my life. I pivoted and dashed toward him. "He's going to kill the dogs!"

For a second Jax didn't move, just stood there with an expression on his face that said, *I have questions about your sanity.*

So much for that connection I thought we had.

"He might have a gun!" I screeched. "He wants the dogs!" I looked over my shoulder and saw Davis spurt out of the alley. Luckily for all of us, the guy wasn't in top shape, so it actually was less of a spurt and more of a sputter.

"My car!" Jax grabbed two of the leashes and hustled the standard poodle and Petey into the back of his SUV. I scrambled into the front passenger seat, pulled the golden onto my lap, and slammed and locked the door as Jax jumped behind the wheel.

"Go, go, go!" I shouted from beneath the dog jockeying for position in the seat.

Jax shoved the car into drive and hit the gas. We flew out of the driveway, bottoming out as we turned onto the street. I grasped the door handle to keep from falling sideways. Jax sped past a few blocks, then cut onto a side street and began to weave his way into a residential neighborhood, driving too fast for the narrow residential streets lined with trees, brick cape cods, and ranch homes. No wonder I heard squealing tires over the phone when I talked to him earlier; the guy drove like he was in a race.

I shoved the golden into the back seat, then checked the road behind us. "You can slow down. No one's back there."

Jax eased off the gas, and glanced at me a couple of times. "What the hell is going on?"

Emotion welled up inside me and I fought the urge to cry. I clasped my hands together in my lap, squeezing my fingers tight as if the pressure could hold back my tears. "He wanted the dogs—"

"Why? Is one of them his?"

"No, no. He's got nothing to do with them. He just came into the shop and *demanded* I give them over."

"He walked in and said, *Gimme the dogs?*" Jax was incredulous. "You didn't leave any others behind, did you?"

I shook my head. "These three were the only ones left."

"That's good." He reached into the back seat and rubbed Petey's neck. "And you have no idea why he wanted the dogs?"

If I told him the truth, then I'd have to tell him about

the diamond ring and who knew if I could trust him. What if he decided he wanted the ring? I stared out the window and tried to think of a logical reason for what had just happened at the shop. We passed a group of children playing chase across the front yards, and I was struck by the fact that even though my life had taken a bizarre twist, it was a typical Friday night for everyone else.

"Some dogs are stolen for dogfighting rings," Jax said when I didn't answer.

"It's not that," I said, almost too emphatically.

"How can you be sure? Do you know that guy?"

"I never saw him before today."

"And he had a gun?"

We pulled up to a stop sign, and Jax looked directly at me. I felt sort of flustery. Partly because the gun thing had actually been my imagination running wild. And partly because he was asking like he really cared about me being threatened by Tom Davis. And, okay, also partly because the way he was looking at me with those *hiding secrets* blue eyes.

"I'm not exactly sure," I said slowly, thinking I should explain why I'd said that earlier. "His torso had a lump like —" *Like the belly of a middle-aged man.* "Well, I mean, when he said to give him the dogs, his eyes got squinty like Clint Eastwood when he says, *Do you feel lucky, punk?* and—"

"Did you actually see a gun?"

Jax pulled away from the stop sign and continued following a circuitous route.

"Well, no." I started feeling a bit hot—and dumb. "But he put his hand under his jacket. And he was so adamant about getting the dogs, I was just afraid he had one." I remembered Davis rubbing his forehead. "Oh, and his other hand...he might have had brass knuckles."

"We should call the cops."

All the events of the past twenty-four hours flashed before my eyes. *Oh no, no, no.* No police yet. If the police got involved, someone would surely appear to be guilty of something illegal—and that someone would surely be me. There were just so many things—that taking the briefcase thing, that breaking and entering the briefcase thing, that missing diamond ring thing. *No police. Not yet.* I shook my head and tried to come up with a good, rational reason to pull Jax back from this idea—an excuse that sounded less insane than all the other stuff I'd just been babbling.

I let out a feeble laugh. "Actually, I may have overreacted. I do that sometimes. I don't really think he had a gun. And...I'm not so sure he had brass knuckles either. The thing is, he was wearing gold rings on all the fingers of his left hand, which made me think of brass knuckles, which made me think of assassins, which, naturally, made me think of guns. And it's been such a long day and I'm tired..." I drew a breath and gave a casual shrug. "And I've always had...an active imagination." Active imagination? I sounded like a raving lunatic.

"Something doesn't feel right. At least we should describe the guy to the police. Maybe he's wanted." Jax checked the rear-view mirror, then adjusted it so he could see the three dogs in a row on the back seat, gazing out the windows like children eagerly waiting to arrive at grandma's house.

Flustered at the direction of our conversation, I said the first thing that came to mind. "When he said he wanted the dogs, my mind went blank." I snapped my fingers to demonstrate how rapidly my gray matter had cleared. "I can't remember his features. All I could offer for a description is that he's male and wearing a tan jacket."

"That's it? I caught the general stuff—big guy, brown hair graying at the temples. But I didn't get a good look at his face. Really, that's all you remember?"

"Afraid so." I nodded to reinforce my words. "The fear must have created, you know, like a memory wipe. Hasn't that ever happened to you?"

"A memory wipe? Can't say that it has."

I rubbed a hand on the back of my neck. "Actually, it never happened to me before today, either. But it happens in shows all the time—especially thrillers and dystopian worlds."

"Yeah, but in dystopian movies, the bad guys wipe your mind of memories, they don't just disappear on their own," Jax pointed out as he drove onto a busier street.

"I think it's kind of a universal reaction to fear and stress." I hoped we weren't going to debate the fine points of dystopian worlds, because I would lose for sure. I was always up for a good movie, but chick flicks were my favorite. There was nothing like a love story to give you that warm, fuzzy feeling—even though the wonderful, romantic stuff that happens in the movies never, and I mean *never,* happens to anyone in—"

I broke off as Jax slammed on the brakes, spun the wheel, and we skidded into the crowded parking lot of a sports bar called *The Fifth Quarter.* As I grabbed for the door handle, I heard the dogs sliding across the back seat, scrambling to keep their balance.

"Sorry," Jax muttered. "Raced go-carts when I was younger. Hard habit to break." Our wheels crunched across the gravel lot. "You can't go back to your car yet—not until we're sure that guy is gone. It's the weekend. I'm hungry...and a drink wouldn't be a bad idea either. What do you think?"

What I thought was, *thank God we were done with dystopian movies and memory wipes.* "Sure," I said enthusias-tically, even though my stomach was such a knot of nerves I didn't want to put anything into it. But sitting in a bar sure beat going back to Flawless Paws too soon and running into Tom Davis again. "I'm not interrupting any plans, am I?"

He shook his head. "Nothing important. I was meeting friends to watch the game, but I'll text them that some-thing else came up."

"That's an understatement." I wondered what Bree and Megan would say about the latest developments. Not just Tom Davis coming back to the shop, but me going out for drinks with two different guys in one week. Never mind that I asked the first one out, and the second one was a complete accident who was now stuck with me for a while because I had spent the afternoon breaking the law.

Bottom line was, two guys for drinks in one week. A record for me.

Forget I said that. Sometimes I am just a moron.

Before going inside, Jax and I took the dogs for a quick walk around the block. I was so worried one of them would poop, I could hardly carry on a conversation. I didn't want to have to explain to Jax why I was monitoring the other two dogs when I had unequivocally said Petey was the guilty party. If he discovered I wasn't one-hundred-percent sure Petey was the culprit, no doubt he would one-hundred-percent insist on taking him home tonight. And I couldn't risk it. I had to find that diamond.

We locked the dogs in the car and Jax assured me they would be safe because his SUV had an alarm system that would go off if anyone tried to break in. Plus, Tom Davis had no idea where we were.

Though The Fifth Quarter was crowded, we were able to nab a couple of seats at the bar. The place had a boisterous vibe—lots happy customers, laughing, talking, watching the baseball game on big screen TVs affixed on every wall.

I ordered a glass of cabernet; Jax ordered a beer and two shots of Jameson Whiskey.

"Two? Rough night already, huh?" I teased, as the

bartender set the shot glasses in front of us and filled them up.

"I've had worse. But I've never had a week come to an end quite like this." Jax threw back one of the shots and handed the other to me. "Bottom's up. This'll settle your nerves a lot faster than wine."

A roar went up in the room, and I glanced at the TV just in time to see two runners cross home plate to take the lead. Some of the crowd began dancing to the stadium music blaring from the speakers. It was yet another contrast in realities for me—them at the height of joy, and me shell-shocked over the events of the last few hours.

I brought the shot glass close to my mouth and inhaled the sweet, strong smell. "I don't really do shots."

He looked at me with those cool blues. "Tonight it's a good idea. Trust me."

For a moment, it felt like the two of us had been swept into some quiet, unreal place where all my troubles and screw-ups didn't exist. I put the shot glass to my lips and quickly finished off the whiskey. Soothing heat cascaded down my throat. "You might be right about the Jameson," I said.

"I'm always right about the Jameson."

I sipped my wine and watched the bartender prepare drinks for other customers—three glasses of red wine, a vodka tonic, two beers. After dropping a lime into the rail drink, he tossed a couple of paper menus our way. "You guys want anything to eat?"

Even though I didn't have one iota of hunger, I picked up the menu to be polite. The place offered all the usual sports bar food: burgers made a million ways, chicken sandwiches, nachos, Buffalo wings, quesadillas, potato skins...and a Cobb salad. After a minute, I realized I was almost salivating at the thought of food. Maybe because I was coming down from the utter terror I had just experienced. Or, more likely because it was well past the dinner hour, and not much could keep me from a decent meal.

"What do you want? Dinner's on me," Jax said, flashing a quick grin.

"A burger sounds good, with Swiss cheese, mushrooms and bacon."

"No salad?" he asked in mock surprise.

"Yeah, this is just the place I would come for a salad," I deadpanned.

Jax chuckled. "Make it two of those burgers," he said to the bartender. "Lettuce and tomato on mine."

"Oh, sure, make me feel guilty. Salad on your burger." I tapped the menu. "I'll have that, too. And fries."

"Onion rings for me. We can trade," Jax said, and we smiled at one another.

There was something so ordinary about the moment, so ordinary and reassuring that it felt extraordinary, like when a tree falls and sunshine streams into a spot that used to be hidden in shadow. I let my gaze wander around the bar, tried to imprint the scene on my mind so I could hang onto this ordinary, extraordinary moment forever.

Maybe it was just my brain's response to the terror I'd gone through at the shop. Or maybe it was the reality of what might have happened if Jax hadn't shown up.

Or maybe it was just being here with Jax.

I touched his arm. "Thanks for refusing to let me keep Petey tonight."

His brows pulled together. "What do you mean?"

"If you had agreed on the phone to let him stay, I would've been at the shop alone. There's no way I could have gotten all three dogs into my car before that guy reached me." I bit my lip. "If you hadn't come back, who knows what might have happened."

Jax took a long pull on his beer and sat silent for a minute. "Petey was my brother's dog."

"Auggie?"

He nodded. "He was in the Marines. Died a year ago in a helicopter crash on a training mission."

"Oh, I'm so sorry," I said softly.

He wrapped both hands around his beer bottle. "Auggie struggled to find his way in the world. Drinking, recreational drugs. Then he found Petey on the street. Couldn't find his owner, so he kept him. The dog gave him purpose. Purpose made him search for direction. And he found it—he was really proud to be a Marine."

"Sounds like he was a good man."

Jax nodded again. "I promised to keep his dog safe until he got back."

That's when I understood. He might not have been

able to protect his younger brother, but he would do whatever it took to protect his brother's dog. "That's why you didn't want to leave him overnight," I said.

"It's all I have of him now." He took another swallow of beer, and after a long moment, changed the subject. "What about the owners of those other two dogs? They probably found the shop wide open and you and their dogs missing. Hell, there's probably a police alert on you already."

I blanched.

"You better call them."

"The police?" I squeaked.

"The dogs' owners."

"Oh, no worries. Both are staying overnight with me. The dogs I mean, not the owners." Omigod, what reason could I give for keeping the dogs overnight without telling him I didn't know which dog swallowed the diamond? "No one is missing them."

"You board pets, too?"

"Exactly," I lied, grateful he'd floated the idea. Except... I probably needed a special license and specific type of facility to keep animals overnight.

"Well, not exactly boarding," I hastily added. "It's more like pet-sitting. Once in a while I do home-boarding for regular customers. I take their dogs to the shop during the day and home with me at night. I make some extra money, and they get peace of mind knowing their dog isn't spending all day in a kennel while they're out of town."

It dawned on me that home-boarding might be a nice

service to offer customers and a way to grow my business. I could easily babysit one or two dogs for a few days at a time. And think how impressed my parents would be when I announced I'd also become a *doggg sitterrrr.*

"You stay busy," Jax said.

Guilt seeped through me over giving one lie after another to the guy who rescued me. I debated whether to come clean and explain what was really going on. And then decided I couldn't risk it. Sometimes giving more information amounted to giving too much information. And too much information in the wrong hands could be my undoing.

Besides, did he really need to know that the missing item was actually a big diamond ring with more carats than a turnip—and not just a simple silver ring? Did he really need to know that I wasn't sure which dog was carrying that sparkly bauble in its belly? Did he really need to know Tom Davis wasn't technically after the dogs, he was after the diamond?

No. No, he did not. Less is the new more.

Thankfully, the bartender set a ketchup bottle and a couple of big napkins on the bar in front of us, ending my overthinking about how much to tell Jax, and opening a space in my brain for me to remember I still didn't have his permission to keep his dog overnight. Which had now become doubly difficult for me to push because of the loss of his brother—and the fact that he knew I was already keeping two other dogs overnight.

"How about another shot of Jameson?" I asked brightly, hoping to ply him with liquor and weaken his resistance. "On me."

"I could be convinced."

When the bartender brought our food, I ordered two more shots. "Bottom's up," I said, holding one out to Jax.

We touched our glasses together, and tossed back the whiskey back at the same time. Jax made a growling noise in his throat and shook his head like a wet dog. Then he squirted some ketchup onto the edge of his plate, scooped an onion ring into the bright red sauce, and took a bite.

I appreciate a man who isn't afraid of ketchup. I once went out with a guy who said that ketchup on French fries was a sign of immaturity. Seriously? He also said that flip-flops were low class and dangling earrings were slutty. My parents thought he was upstanding, but I got rid of him.

The baseball game played on the wall above us, and I half watched it as I bit into my burger—so juicy, I had to wipe my chin—and tried to figure out what to do about Petey. Obviously, the only way Jax would let me keep the dog overnight was if he trusted me. And the only way he would trust me was if we knew each other better. I pushed a couple of fries into my mouth and mulled over how to begin.

"So, Jax, what do you do?" I said at last.

"I'm a ranger."

Both brothers were military? "Like in the Army?"

"No, like in the forest. National Park Service."

This lead-footed racecar driver was actually a naturalist in disguise? Not that I minded, it seemed really interesting—just incongruous, in a good way. I pictured him in the woods, rugged and masculine: hiking boots, green pants, gray shirt, and a Smokey the Bear hat.

Somehow, I just knew it wouldn't impress the old folks back home. I wondered if my mother would say *forrrest raaaanger* like she said *doggg groooomer*.

What was wrong with me? This wasn't a date. Jax was my rescuer, not a romance option. Who cared whether his job would impress my parents? Certainly not me. "That's awesome. I've never met a park ranger—outside of a park, I mean. What do you do exactly?"

"Whatever needs to be done. Patrol the park, help people, give tours..."

"Do you get to hang out at the top of those wooden towers?"

He snorted out a laugh. "Everyone's favorite question. Fire lookouts are usually manned by volunteers."

Oh. I took a couple more bites of burger and mulled over how cool it would be to volunteer as a fire lookout person. All the peace and quiet up there, birds tweeting, the wind rustling the trees. Overall, it would be a pretty awesome gig. At least until there was a fire. But even then you'd be saving lives. And you'd literally be able to say that what you do at your job is put out fires all day—and it would be true.

I was about to make that joke to Jax when my phone

vibrated on the counter and I swiped the screen to open a text message from Bree. She and Megan were probably happy at Happy Hour by now, and checking in to see how I was doing with the dogs. I glanced at the message, then slowly read each word again: *Colin dead. Channel 4. Now.*

EIGHT

A CHUNK OF BURGER LODGED IN MY THROAT, AND I TRIED TO wash it down with a swallow of cabernet, almost choking as the whole mess crawled its way to my stomach. After reading Bree's text one more time, I waved a frantic hand at the bartender and pointed to the television above the bar. "Can we change the channel? Can we switch to—?"

The words, *Breaking News,* splashed across the screen and were quickly replaced by the a pretty male reporter, mouth moving soundlessly as closed captioning scrolled along the bottom saying a man had been pulled from the river. A grainy photograph confirmed that the man in question was the same one I'd met at breakfast, the man I'd had drinks with, the man whose briefcase used to be in my possession, and whose ring still was. Sort of.

I could hardly breathe. They'd pulled Colin's body out

of the river? My hunger evaporated. Thoughts charged like machine gun fire through my brain.

Colin was dead. *Colin was dead.* Obviously, he had a good excuse for not coming back into the restaurant last night—maybe someone had been after him. Obviously, he didn't go to Zurich like Tom Davis said. Why had Davis lied? Oh no, no, no. Did Tom Davis kill Colin and push him in the river? Oh. My. God. He killed Colin for the jewelry and the turnip diamond—and then discovered Colin didn't even have it. My mind flashed back to our confrontation at Flawless Paws, when Davis snarled, "Get me the damn dogs." Colin didn't even look like a jewel thief, but Tom Davis sure looked like an enforcer.

What had I gotten myself into?

Easy, easy, I didn't need to jump to conclusions. Maybe Colin fell in or...went for a swim. *In the middle of the night?* I yelled at myself. What if Davis grabbed Colin when he left Sullivan's to make that call, and that's why he never came back? And no one spotted the body until tonight.

Why did this stuff always happen to me? Why was my life such a disaster?

Thank God I hadn't introduced him to my family yet.

I rubbed a hand on the back of my neck. What was wrong with me? A man was dead, and I responded with relief that my parents hadn't met him yet.

Jax followed my gaze to the television. "Someone you know?"

I shook my head as the ball game filled the screen again.

"What channel did you want?" The bartender pointed the remote at the TV.

"Never mind, this one's fine." I fired off a one-word reply to Bree: *Yes.*

Something had gone wrong. Terribly wrong. And now I was in possession of a dead man's diamond ring. A big, fat, diamond that was probably worth a fortune.

Or, more accurately, I was in possession of the dog that was in possession of the diamond.

But why waste time quibbling over semantics? Especially when, based on the news report, I now had a bigger problem. I could have been one of the last people to see Colin alive. Maybe even the last one—besides the killer. So, not only could I be arrested for breaking and entering and theft, there was a very reasonable chance I could now be detained as a murder suspect. Woohoo.

I set down my burger and all I could think of was the cow that died to make that burger possible. Just an ordinary cow going along minding its own business, eating grass, chewing its cud, taking a nap once in a while...and then, boom, he's a hamburger. I empathized completely.

"Hey...you okay?" Jax asked.

The phone vibrated with another text from Bree: *Are you home? Megan and I are coming over.*

I sent her the name of the bar, then looked into Jax's

perceptive, piercing eyes. "The truth of the matter is, I think I'm in big trouble."

He set his elbows on the bar, put an onion ring in his mouth, and washed it down with a swallow of beer. Based on his expression, he'd already figured out there was more to my story than I'd shared. "What's going on?"

I took a deep breath and dove in, explaining how my parents forty-fifth anniversary party was coming up and the girls and I had been trying to—oh, God, I couldn't believe I had to say this out loud—meet eligible men at hotel continental breakfast...by pretending we were on business trips of our own. Abashed, I kept talking, describing how I'd met Colin and gotten his briefcase. How Phinneas broke into the briefcase and we lost the diamond. How I'd given the briefcase to Tom Davis because he claimed to work with Colin. How he'd come back to get the diamond and threatened the dogs. And how I had just discovered that Colin, the man I thought would prove to my parents that I wasn't a total screw-up, was now a dead man featured on *Breaking News*.

"It's not much of a stretch," I said, "to see how the police would consider me a person-of-interest in this whole case because even I think I seem like a person-of-interest."

And then, believe it or not, I shut up.

Jax's brows pulled together as if he were trying to decide whether I was telling the truth—or if I was disturbed and hallucinatory. "How big is this diamond?" he finally asked.

Really? That was his first question? The most important thing he needed to know? I held my thumb and index finger about half an inch apart.

The corners of his mouth twitched. "And you're saying that sparkling rock is in one of the dogs in my car?"

"That would be correct."

He checked his watch. "Oh, will you look at the time? I have to get going. I'll give you a call if the diamond shows up."

I started to sputter. Jax barked out a laugh, but I didn't smile. This thing may be funny to him, but it sure wasn't to me.

"Sorry. I couldn't resist." He reined in his grin. "Truthfully, though, there's really a diamond ring inside one of those dogs?"

"Yes, a diamond that belongs to a *dead man*. And not only was I one of the last people to see him alive, I broke into his briefcase and, some might say, took the big diamond." I put my elbows on the bar and dropped my head into my hands. "It's so unbelievable. This stuff never happens to anyone else. It's exactly why my parents think I'm a screw-up. And you know, sometimes I think they may be right."

Jax sobered. "Don't jump to conclusions." He finished off his burger and washed it down with the rest of his beer. "Let's start with that Tom Davis guy. He has motive—

maybe he just wanted the diamond for himself. What exactly did he say about it?"

"That it was about to be sold. There was no time to wait."

"Hmm. To who?"

"He didn't share his business dealings with me when he was demanding the dogs." My words came out more harshly than I intended. I closed my eyes for a second. "Sorry."

"Don't worry about it." He drummed his fingers on the bar, thinking. "So...you went up to a *complete stranger* and asked to share a breakfast table?"

"It was crowded," I said defensively. "All the tables were taken, so it didn't seem that odd."

"Then he asked you for a date?"

"Technically...I asked him."

"You asked him for a date."

"You don't have to say it like I was desperate. Because I wasn't. And I'm not." Which was a lie, but I really didn't want him to think of me as desperate. "I just needed an acceptable guy to take to my parent's forty-fifth anniversary party." *Oh, God, I sounded desperate.*

"Sorry. I was just trying to see if there was more to this story than *girl meets boy, girl loses diamond, boy gets killed.* So you ask him for a date and then what?" Jax asked.

I huffed. "We went out. Isn't that how it usually works? Girl meets boy, one asks the other out, they go on a date."

"Well, yeah. But not typically at continental breakfast." He sat back in his chair and eyed me dubiously.

How could he not believe me? Who could make up a story this ludicrous? Tears pricked at the back of my eyes. If Jax didn't believe me, and he had been there for the chase through the parking lot, the cops would never believe me. I would be on my own in this nightmare.

"Allie!" Bree squeezed between my bar stool and Jax's and wrapped me in a quick hug.

I'd never been so happy to see her.

"Omigod, I can't believe this is happening," she said. "You finally meet a guy and he's, well, uh...passed to the other side already. What are the odds?" She lowered her voice, barely moving her lips as she asked, "Any sign of the ring yet?"

I sighed. "Things have gone from bad to worse. Wait until you hear it."

Megan came up on my other side and put an arm around my shoulder. "Bree told me what happened with the dogs and the diamond," she whispered. "It's really shocking about Colin...but I don't think you have anything to worry about. As soon as we get the ring back, we'll just give it to that associate of his—"

"Tom Davis," Bree interjected.

"Right. And then you can forget about the whole thing."

Bree patted my shoulder. "More important, though,

you know what they say when you fall off a horse, the best thing to do is get right back on again."

A hysterical laugh tried to bubble out of my throat and I swallowed it down. "This isn't as simple as falling—"

"Figuratively speaking," Bree said. "Listen, listen, I have a great idea. Monday, you and I are going to the Franklin Inn. We're getting right back on the horse."

Jax leaned into our discussion like he was one of the girls. "To meet single men at continental breakfast?"

Megan lay one of her imperious attorney stares on him. "Who the hell is this? And what does he know?"

"Everything. He knows everything." I drank some more wine. "Megan, Bree—this is Jax. I gave his dog a bath today. And then he saved my life."

Bree reached out to shake his hand. Her gaze swiveled between Jax and me. "The dog saved your life?" she asked.

"No, Jax did."

"Literally saved your life? I feel like we're missing some information," Megan said.

I nodded. "You are. After Bree left today—"

"Does this have anything to do with—" Bree lowered her voice. "The diamond?"

Megan held up a hand. "Okay, enough talk at the bar. Too many ears. Let's get a table." She ordered a bottle of pinot noir for the three of us, and a beer for Jax, then perused the busy room. "We need a spot where we can't easily be overheard."

"Really? Saved your life?" Bree said under her breath to me.

"As you say, figuratively speaking," I said. "Then again, maybe literally, too. With everything that's going on, who knows?"

"Shush," Megan ordered.

Jax raised his brows.

"She's a lawyer. Used to taking control," I said.

"And being right," Bree added. "Sometimes it gets old."

A few minutes later, we were settled at a small round table in a corner, under a wall-mounted speaker that was piping music out just loud enough to create a sound barrier. If someone wanted to hear our conversation, they'd really have to work at it. We looked at one another for a minute, then Jax said to Megan, "Before we go any further, I need you to tell me what you three are up to."

"I already told you," I said.

"I need to hear it from someone else."

So, Megan matter-of-factly described how we formed the Continental Breakfast Club to meet single guys. "It was my idea, but I'm not convinced it's as brilliant as Bree and Allie think. Sure, Allie met Colin the first day," she said. "But now there's a bizarre twist, with Colin up the river, figuratively speaking, and the ring missing. Still, things have a way of working themselves out, so I'm not worried...much."

Jax gestured at me. "Tell them about tonight."

I quickly recounted what happened when Davis

returned to the shop. "I'll bet Tom Davis had something to do with Colin's death. Think about it, Bree. When he said Colin was in Zurich—"

"He might already have been—" She made a slashing motion across her throat with her right hand. "Allie, what if he killed Colin for that diamond? And now he knows you have it. I have to tell you—"

"I know, I know. I'm next," I said in a frenzied voice. "Don't you think I've thought of that already?"

Bree set down her glass of wine. "Calm down. That wasn't what I was going to say. After I got home this afternoon, I Googled diamonds. Found a site that listed movie stars' wedding rings and what they're worth."

I could already tell the information wasn't going to make me happy. "Do I really want to know this?"

"Your diamond could be worth a million dollars. Maybe more." Bree took a drink of wine as though it would help her come to grips with a math value that had so many zeros in it.

"It's not *my* diamond," I said sharply.

"If that rock is worth a million, it explains a lot," Jax said.

"That's only if it's flawless," Bree hastened to add. "Otherwise it might not be worth that much. It all depends on the four Cs—cut, clarity, color, and carat weight."

What. Ever. I finished my wine and refilled my glass.

"Flawless, almost flawless. Only the guy with the jeweler's loupe can tell the difference," Jax said.

"Someone wants that diamond bad—and that's all that matters."

"Was Tom Davis armed?" Megan asked.

"I'm not sure. He didn't pull out a gun or anything," I said.

"Don't forget the brass knuckles." Jax's eyes sparkled, and I had the distinct impression he was poking fun.

"He had brass knuckles?" Bree asked as though enthralled by the idea.

I threw a sheepish glance at Jax. "He had a bunch of gold rings on one hand that, someone...say, a person unfamiliar with weapons...might mistake for brass knuckles...if that person was under extreme stress."

"Maybe they were brass knuckles designed to masquerade as rings. Sophisticated brass knuckles for upscale assassins," Bree said helpfully.

Oh, now that reply would certainly help my image in Jax's eyes.

"Do you think we should call the police?" Megan asked.

A roar went up from the crowd and I startled. For a fraction of a ridiculous second, I thought everyone been eavesdropping and were voicing their support for calling the cops. A runner crossed home plate on the television, and I gave myself a mental shake. I had to get hold of myself; jittery nerves would not be an asset moving forward in this mess.

Once the cheering and whistling and clapping died down, Jax looked at each of us in turn.

"I know I'm the new guy and maybe there's something I'm missing, but the way this looks to me...if you call the cops, it might not go so well for Allie. What exactly do you tell them?" he asked. "That Allie might be the last person to see Colin before he died under suspicious circumstances? That she took his briefcase home and broke into it, removed a valuable diamond ring, and now it's *missing*? Oh wait, she thinks a dog ate it but isn't sure which one, and now some guy is after her and possibly threatening to kill the dogs?"

"You don't think they'll believe it?" Bree asked.

"I don't believe it and I know it's true," Megan said.

"I'm not going to the police," I said firmly. I pictured myself in an interrogation room, a glaring white light blinding my vision as I tried to make a group of detectives believe my story. "I'd be locked up and charged before morning."

"Either that, or they'll think you're a crackpot," Jax said. "That you saw the story about Colin being pulled from the river on the news, and embellished it with a new angle about diamonds."

"In other words, they wouldn't believe me anyway."

Jax inclined his head.

"There's no point in going to the cops until we actually have the diamond," Megan said.

"Couldn't we have the dogs X-rayed to find out which

one swallowed it?" Jax asked. "At least then we'd only have to watch one."

I proudly raised my hand and beamed at him. "Way ahead of you. X-rays are scheduled for first thing in the morning."

"Why wait?" Megan asked, while Jax and Bree nodded agreement.

I felt a bit ganged-up on. "Maybe you haven't noticed, but I was working all day."

"There are after-hours vets." Jax took a pull on his beer.

"Yeah, but they're expensive. Just because I own my own business doesn't mean I'm getting rich." Far from it, actually. For some reason, people who have no problem paying megabucks to get their own hair cut think it's highway robbery to pay a reasonable fee for a dog cut—a service that includes not just a full-body cut, but also a bath, nail trim and, ack, anal gland expression.

I rubbed my thumb and fingers together as if burnishing dollar bills. "X-rays of three dogs at the emergency clinic won't come cheap."

"Hold that thought, I'll find out." Megan picked up her phone and went outside to call the vet clinic. She was back in minutes. "Drink up, everyone. They said we can come over immediately. We'll have an answer tonight."

I considered my MasterCard bill that was due next week. "How much?"

"Doesn't matter."

"No, it does. Really it does." I pictured the long row of

charges on my bill, most of which wouldn't get paid off this month.

"It doesn't matter because we're splitting it three ways." Megan held a hand toward Bree. "Right?"

"This is a cost incurred by the Continental Breakfast Club," Bree said in an official tone. "All members share expenses equally."

Jax raised his beer bottle. "And since it was my dog that knocked the diamond loose in the first place, count me in too. A four-way split."

My throat tightened and I gave them a watery grin. What would I do without my friends?

Since there were only three chairs in the waiting room at the emergency vet clinic, the young female assistant rolled out a desk chair so we could all have a seat. The walls were lined with framed Norman Rockwell prints of kids with dogs and cats—homey, happy pictures intended to ease the fear that accompanied an emergency room visit.

I filled out the consent forms on a clipboard while Megan reiterated to the vet what she had earlier said on the phone: that one of the dogs had swallowed a ring with a big cubic zirconia and we needed to find out which dog to monitor. It was such a relief to let someone else do the talking for a change and just blithely go along. The vet assured her he could probably get the X-rays done without anesthetizing the dogs, then he and the assistant took all three dogs into the back room.

"Why didn't you just tell him the truth?" Jax asked Megan under his breath.

She shrugged. "No need for him to know. The fewer people aware of the truth, the better. Just holding our cards close to our collective chests."

"Plus, if he knew it was a real diamond," Bree added, "what's to stop him from deciding he wants to keep it himself?"

"Yeah, but how would he get it?" Jax asked.

Bree tapped a finger against her lips. "Maybe...he'd say the diamond was about to perforate the dog's bowel and he needed to perform emergency surgery. Once it was out, he'd keep the real one and give us a cubic zirconia."

Megan barked out a laugh. "Where's he going to get a cubic zirconia ring on a Friday night?"

"Everyone else has been lying to get at that diamond," I said cynically. "Why should the vet be any different?" I crossed the waiting room to study a cat anatomy chart on the wall even though I had no interest in cat anatomy.

Megan and Bree began to page through pet magazines. Jax dropped his head against the chair back and closed his eyes. I sat down again, but nervous energy propelled me to my feet a minute later.

I gazed out the window at the summer night and tried not to think about what had happened to Colin. I examined the shelves of supplies—natural dog food and treats and shampoo. I read the dog and cat adoption notices on the bulletin board. I tried to puzzle out what Tom Davis was all about. In short, I did everything I could to avoid thinking about the million dollar diamond—okay, the maybe million dollar diamond—that I had lost.

Minutes passed until almost half an hour was gone. Megan checked at her watch. "At least we'll only have one dog to worry about soon."

"And some guy who might have a gun," Bree added.

"No, no, no. I never actually saw a gun," I said. "I was just...projecting."

"Projecting or not, here's what we know." Jax stood and stretched his back. "A man is dead. And Tom Davis was threatening—at least toward the dogs. Sure, he could have been bluffing, but we'd be stupid to assume that. And we'd be stupid to assume he didn't have anything to do with Colin's death. Better prepared than surprised."

"But if Tom Davis did kill Colin..." I pressed my back against the counter. "Giving him the diamond may not help me. What if he's afraid I can identify him? What if he wants to make sure I'm out of the way for good?" I scrubbed my hands over my face. "And my family. What if he goes after my family? Omigod I'm such a—"

"No, you're not," Jax said.

Bree and Megan simultaneously swiveled toward him. The room was so quiet, I could hear the tick of the old, round analog clock on the wall.

"You're not a screw-up," he said.

"Thanks, but you hardly have the experience with me to make that call."

"I think I can identify a screw-up when I see one."

"Promise me you'll tell my parents that when I'm—"

The door from the back room opened and the vet stepped out, the epitome of personality plus. "I've got probably the best news you could ask for."

I brought my hands up in jubilant fists. "You got it out?"

"Better than that. It was never in. The X-rays show nothing out of the ordinary. None of those dogs swallowed your ring."

NINE

WHAT? "*WHAT?*" I FELT LIKE I'D AWAKENED FROM A nightmare only to discover reality was even worse than the dream. If the diamond wasn't in any of the dogs, where was it?

"The X-rays don't show anything unusual. None of them swallowed the cubic zirconia."

"How can that be?" Jax asked, flabbergasted.

The vet lifted gave a shrug. "Maybe it rolled under a piece of furniture."

"We searched everywhere. We couldn't have missed it." Bree stood. "I was there, I saw it happen. It flew through the air, glittering. Fell to the floor among all these little treats and then—" She twirled an invisible magic wand. "—the dogs gobbled everything up and it was gone. Just gone."

The vet stuck his hands in the pockets of his white

coat. "I don't know what to say. All three dogs are clean. I was worried it might be stuck in the intestinal tract and we would need to operate to get it out. Could have been really dangerous. But, luck is definitely on your side."

He thought I was lucky? I almost laughed. *Cursed* was more like it. If we couldn't find that diamond, my life would become utter shambles. "We searched everywhere," I muttered, as though repeating Bree's words would somehow change the outcome.

"Look at the bright side." The vet went behind the counter and scribbled some notes in the chart. "How much can it cost to replace a fake diamond ring? Twenty dollars? Surgery might have put you back a thousand. Think of it this way, you dodged a bullet."

"Yeah, Allie, cheer up." Jax put an arm around my shoulders and gave me a squeeze. "At least you didn't lose a real diamond that size."

"You're right. I really am lucky," I said with forced enthusiasm.

The vet assistant came around the corner with the dogs, all three tugging at their leashes, eager to escape the clinic. "Here they are, none the worse for the wear," she said, passing leashes to Megan, Bree, and Jax.

I paid for a small bag of dog food and the X-rays with my credit card, then followed the others outside into the warm night, four crestfallen adults accompanied by three joyful dogs. As soon as the clinic door clunked shut, we started talking at once. The closer we got to our cars, the louder our voices became.

Bree let out a screech. "Maybe his stomach acid dissolved it and there isn't a diamond anymore."

We gaped at her, speechless. Dumbstruck.

"Bree, did you not pay attention in high school earth science?" I said. "Diamonds are the hardest natural substance known to man. Six hours in stomach acid would not dissolve a diamond."

She gave me a smug nod, one that implied I would soon be bowing down before her cleverness. "Unless it was a paste diamond," she said. "Maybe it wasn't real. The stomach acids could have dissolved the paste." She stuck out one hand, then closed it into a fist. "Now you see it, now you don't."

"Paste diamonds are made out of leaded glass." Megan said in bored monotone. "Not that white goo you use in kindergarten art projects."

"Where do you learn this stuff?" I asked, impressed.

"Are you sure?" Bree looked unconvinced.

Megan groaned. "Trust me. They're leaded glass and wouldn't dissolve."

Confirmation enough for me. "Okay, the diamond didn't dissolve. And none of the dogs swallowed it. Which means it's at the shop somewhere. We need to search Flawless Paws again."

"You think it's safe to go back?" Bree asked.

"It better be. It's been hours since we left." Jax opened

the hatch on his SUV and Petey jumped inside. "If that guy has any brains, he'll know Allie isn't going back there with the dogs tonight. Not after what happened."

"Or rather, what you prevented from happening. Thank you." I smiled at Jax and realized there wasn't any reason for him to stay involved any longer. His dog had been cleared of wrong-doing; the two of them could go home.

"Just glad I showed up when I did."

I held up my wrist to show him my watch. "It's not very late. If you hurry you can probably catch the rest of the game with those friends you blew off," I said brightly, though I wasn't feeling anything of the sort.

"Just in time for the seventh-inning stretch," he said. "Okay, girls. Great meeting you all. Good luck with...everything. I hope you find that diamond."

As he drove away, disappointment filtered through me. Somehow, just having him around had made it feel like things might turn out all right.

Megan drove through the alley, across the parking lot and past Flawless Paws as the three of us peered out the windows, on the alert for people or cars that seemed out of place. Everything was deserted; my Civic was the only vehicle even remotely close to the building.

She pulled into a parking space at the far end of the lot

so there was a clear view of both the entrance to the alley and the street in front of my shop. "Let's sit here and watch a minute," she said, shutting off the headlights, "Just to make sure we're alone."

I couldn't have agreed more. There was a big difference between talking about going into the shop and actually doing it. The three of us sat silent and unmoving in the darkness, gazes glued on the shop, fear weaving through our stomachs, tension coiling tightly around us like a boa constrictor.

Which is why, when another car whipped into the parking space right next to us, we all screamed like banshees heralding death. "Get us out of here," Bree cried.

Megan turned the key in the ignition. A face loomed outside my window, and I shrank back against the two dogs, shrieking, "Drive, drive!"

Recognition gave me a knuckle rap to the head. "Jax?"

Megan shut off the engine. I lowered the window and cleared my raw throat. "Oh my God, what are you doing here?"

"Scaring the shit out of you, apparently. Sorry." He got into the backseat with me.

"What about the ball game? And your friends?" My heart was still pounding from misplaced terror.

"They won't care." He looked at me across the interior of the car, the planes of his face accentuated by shadows from the streetlights, his blue eyes mysterious in the darkness. "Just because I think Davis should be gone by now, doesn't mean he actually is. I didn't want you to go in there alone."

I flushed with warmth.

"She won't be alone. Megan and I will be there," Bree said.

Shut up, Bree, my mind whispered.

"I think it would be better if some of us stayed out here, standing watch," Jax said. "In case someone is already inside. Or comes back."

"I thought the same thing," Megan said. "Let's break into two groups."

"Agreed. How about if Allie and I go into the shop." Jax smiled at me. "Megan and Bree, you two keep the car running, the doors locked, and your eyes open."

"Allie, call my phone before you go in," Megan said. "I'll stay on the line until you confirm the shop is clear. That way if anyone is inside, I'll know instantly and we can call the police from Bree's phone."

"Perfect," Jax said.

"Sounds good." I ran a hand down the silky back of the golden retriever. "But if anything goes wrong, you guys get out of here. I don't want anyone, including dogs, getting hurt over my mistakes."

"Blah, blah, blah. Is someone talking? Because I can't make out a word." Bree cupped her hands around her ears, pretending like she was trying to hear.

"How many times do I have to repeat myself? This is the Continental Breakfast Club," Megan said. "Our motto is, *Leave no woman behind.* So let's quit talking and get moving, shall we?"

Jax and I went into Flawless Paws through the main entrance, with me giving Megan a commentary via phone, every step of the way. I flipped on the double light switch inside the door and the main room exploded into brightness.

Jax blinked a couple of times. "Welcome to the surface of the sun."

"I have to be able to see what I'm doing when I'm working."

"With wattage like that, even the people down the block will be able to see what you're doing."

After confirming that no one was in the shop, we locked both doors, and ended the call with Megan. My gaze flicked over the back room—the desk on one side, a row of coat hooks for work smocks and outerwear on the other, and a three-tiered wall of kennels along the back. Though the main room had been wired for ultimate light, this area was definitely the poor sister; its two single-bulb fixtures created plenty of shadowed areas, especially at night.

I moved into the doorway between the two rooms and opened my arms wide. "I was here," I said to Jax. "Bree was about where you are. I pulled the diamond from my pocket and held it out to Bree like this..." I demonstrated, palm up. "Then Petey nudged my hand and everything went flying." I threw my arms up like I was tossing confetti.

"Nudged?"

"Okay, *rammed.*"

"That sounds more like Petey." Jax turned on his phone flashlight and dropped to his knees to examine the old wooden floor. While some of the planks still fit together as tightly as the day they were laid a hundred years ago, there were serious gaps between others.

He stuck his pinkie into one of the gaps. "It's probably wedged between two floorboards somewhere. Old buildings always end up with lots of openings as they settle. It's how the mice get in."

"Jax!" I peered at a dark corner, visions of rodents with long tails running through my mind, then whipped open a desk drawer to get a flashlight so I could help search.

Jax sat back on his heels and pointed at the wall of kennels. "Desperate question. What about these cages? They seem flush to the floor, but...is there any chance it could it have slid underneath? Can we move them?"

"They're attached to both the floor and wall." I pushed against the kennels to demonstrate their immovability, then punched the toe of my shoe against the kick plate. "There's no way for anything to get underneath either."

He exhaled slowly. "We've searched every inch of this room twice."

A knot tightened my throat. What in the hell happened to that diamond ring?

"Are you sure you weren't in the main room?" Jax asked.

"I may have all sorts of other issues but my memory is intact," I said a bit snippily. "Bree and I were definitely back here."

"Just wanted to make sure. Since you had that memory wipe thing happen."

Oh yeah, that. My cheeks flooded with color. Thank God the lighting was so bad Jax probably wouldn't notice.

"I don't know where else to look," he said.

Tears pressed into my eyes and I squeezed the bridge of my nose with two fingers to hold them back. "What am I going to do?" I said in a thick voice. "There's no way out. Tom Davis wants that diamond and I lost it. I've tried so hard to be responsible, to get my life together...but no matter what I do, something always goes wrong."

"No, not always." Suddenly Jax's arms were around me and his hands were smoothing my hair. "You're a smart, beautiful woman who's hit a rough patch. Just a rough patch and it's going to be all right. Really."

I could feel him breathing, the heat of his body against mine, and I didn't pull away because I felt so safe in his arms. "I wish that were true," I murmured. And then, oh God, I snuffled. Against his chest. I didn't mean to, but my lids were already awash, which was making my nose stuffy, and a snuffle sneaked out before I could stop it.

How mortifying.

"We'll make it true," Jax repeated.

I wanted to believe him, really I did. But he'd known me less than ten hours. He may have all the best intentions, but he had no idea how often things in my life went ker-plop without warning. I mean, consider Colin. One night ago, he seemed like a great guy who wanted to get to know me, and now he was...singing with the angels. One night ago, I thought I was on a path toward finding the kind of boyfriend who might lead to the kind of husband that would make my parents start treating me like an adult. And tonight? I was running for my life—in the arms of another man.

If that wasn't the title of a country western song, it should be: *Running for my Life in the Arms of another Man.*

Anyway, as my mind was whirling like a high-strung Yorkshire terrier begging for a treat, I pulled back to look up at Jax and say something about getting back to searching. But before even a word could pass my lips, his mouth was on mine. *He was kissing me.*

After a shocked moment during which my brain emptied itself of any coherent thought, I leaned into him and kissed him back, this stranger I'd met only that morning, this man who had somehow become my friend, and— the kiss deepened and my brain went further into new territory—maybe even *the one who was meant to be.*

No.

No. No. No. No. No. I might gone to continental breakfast to meet men, but after the Colin debacle, I could not be so pitifully desperate that I ascribed *the one who was meant to be* to every man I met.

Besides, Jax couldn't possibly be *the one who was meant*

to be. He was a forest ranger. Strike that. *Forrrest raaaanger.* He might be the nicest guy in the world, but I knew that forest ranger just wouldn't pass the parent test.

The thought was so disheartening, I took several steps back to put space between us, to force his kiss from my mind, to refocus our attention on the disaster at hand. "Where do you think we should search now?" I turned a slow circle.

Jax shook his head, his expression unreadable. "I don't know. Think again about when it happened. Do you remember anything new? How about later? Could a dog owner have come into the back room and found it? A cleaning person?"

I pressed my fingers to my forehead as if the action would work like a computer *on/off* switch, loading my thoughts in the proper order so I could remember every byte of that afternoon, beginning with the moment the diamond went airborne.

"No. The only cleaning person is me. And no one ever comes in the back room. Well, except Tom Davis when he chased me outside." I aimed my flashlight beam on the door to the alley. "Unless... Jax, what if Davis came back in the shop after we escaped and found it himself? Maybe he's got the diamond already, and we're off the hook!" I felt a tentative stirring of elation, but braced myself for Jax's take on my theory.

"It doesn't fit," he said, shaking his head. "You told him one of the dogs ate it. So it makes more sense that he'd jump in his car and try to follow us. Even if he did come back into the shop, what are the odds he'd just happen upon the ring when it's so well hidden you and Bree couldn't even find it—and you were actually looking for it?"

My euphoria evaporated.

"Which also means it's pretty unlikely someone else came into the shop while it was unlocked and found the ring," he said.

Oh, happy day. I hadn't even gone that far with my speculation.

Jax shoved his hands into the front pockets of his jeans. "Here's what I'm afraid happened. It's an old building. Over time, walls shift, floors move, cracks open where they never were before. I think the ring landed in one of those openings. God only knows where it is now."

"Are you saying we have to tear this place apart?" Despair was too weak a word for what I was feeling.

"Even if we took the building apart piece-by-piece, I'm not sure we'd find it."

I gaped at him, my thoughts circling like water in a sink, coming ever closing to slipping down the drain. Was there no escaping destiny? That damn Continental Breakfast Club. If I survived this, if we were able to get Tom Davis off my back, I would never again lament the fact that I couldn't meet a good guy. Never. *Ever.*

Well, maybe not quite *ever*, but I would never again go

to continental breakfast with the goal of trying to meet a man.

Well, maybe not *never,* but okay, at least I would never go to continental breakfast at the Tucker Point Hotel again.

"To tell the truth, I'm not sure what we should do," Jax said.

"So, where does this leave me? Tom Davis wants that diamond and we can't find it. *Jax, what do I do?*" I knew I sounded agitated; *I was* agitated. And running out of hope. My palms were damp, my heart was trying to pound its way out of my chest, my breath was coming in short bursts like my lungs had become a bellows. I was *zombies-are-in-the-next-room* terrified. What was going to happen to me?

Jax perused the room through narrowed eyes. "Let's go see if Bree remembers anything else."

We locked the shop and walked across the parking lot, shoulders drooping like two doleful basset hounds dragging their long ears on the ground. We were so dejected, I don't think either of us bothered to care whether Tom Davis came back and found us. After all, he could do his worst and he still wouldn't get the diamond.

High above us, a bright sliver of moon and a million stars peeked in and out from behind overstuffed clouds tumbling across the obsidian sky. On any other night, I would have been captivated by that beautiful sight and thinking it might be an incredible backdrop to kissing Jax Kelly again. Tonight it was just a reminder that nothing lasts forever. And whatever can go wrong, will. You know, the usual uplifting proverbs.

As we neared Megan's car, the front doors popped open and the girls jumped out. The dogs tried to follow, determined not to be left out of the next step of the adventure.

"No!" Megan commanded and closed the door to keep the golden inside.

Bree wasn't faring as well. "Halt! Stay! Now listen to me, you're not coming out," she was saying as though the dogs would understand.

Finally she straight-armed the standard poodle and pushed the door shut. Both dogs popped their heads out the half-open windows like clowns in old jack-in-the-box toys.

"Did you find it?" Bree sounded like she was already ducking for cover, afraid of the answer.

I let out a dispirited laugh. "No. Missing in action. Remember how I got such a great deal on rent because the space was sort of rough? Well now I'm paying for it."

"Just guessing here," Jax said, "But the only thing that makes sense is that it rolled into a crack between the floorboards and down into the framing of the building."

"Oh God, no," Megan said.

I dropped my head back to gaze up at the stunning night sky and wished I was on a rocket to the moon.

"Bree, do you remember anything else that might help?" Jax asked. "Anything?"

She thought for a long moment, then sagged against

the car. "Nothing. You know, maybe we should dump the idea of finding the diamond and just go to the police." She held up a hand to silence us before anyone could protest. "Sure, we're guilty of losing Colin's diamond. And yeah, okay, we actually have no proof there ever was a diamond. But Colin is dead. And Tom Davis threatened you and the dogs, and for all we know, he killed Colin."

Hard to believe that less than two days ago, I had only just met Colin and thought things were looking up. What was that saying? *What a difference a day makes.*

No kidding. No friggin' kidding.

TEN

"IF WE GO TO THE POLICE NOW, I STILL HAVE THE SAME problem I had two hours ago," I said. "Without the diamond, I sound like a crazy person trying to capitalize on Colin's death to get fifteen minutes of fame."

Jax stepped to the car window to rub Petey's cheeks and get a sloppy lick across the nose in return. "Just as bad, what if they believe some of what you tell them—and think you're lying about the rest? What if they accept that Colin did have a briefcase full of jewelry? But think you're the person who killed him to get it."

Bree let out a sharp laugh. "Well, then, she'll just get charged with theft and murder."

"Exactly," I said. "I don't want to go to the cops and have it backfire on me."

Megan rested her hip against her car and crossed her arms. "I could find you a really good criminal defense attorney, but—" She rubbed her forehead. "The whole Tom Davis thing is another sticking point. Right now we can't even prove he exists. It's a common name, and we have no phone number, no license plate number, no photo of him—"

"Allie can't even describe him," Jax put in.

"Really?" Bree asked, shocked. "I remember pretty much everything. S and P, RHL, SL, NMM, SA, a little scar on his forehead, six foot, two-forty—Allie I can't believe you don't remember."

Omigod, Bree, *know when to say when*. I rolled my eyes and translated: "S and P—salt and pepper hair, RHL—receding hair line, SL—skinny lips, NMM—not much muscle, SA—saggy ass..."

Jax looked astounded.

"You really can't remember?" Bree asked.

Of course I remember, I wanted to say. *I'm not totally oblivious.* But if I admitted that now, Jax would realize I lied about my memory issue. I debated what to do. Would it be better for him to think of me as a dimwit...or a liar? All sides of my mind voted for dimwit. "I think the stress caused a memory wipe," I said.

Bree's mouth dropped open. "A memory wipe?" She sounded fascinated enough to blow the thing into a major discussion. "I thought that only happened in the movies."

I gave an almost imperceptible shake of my head and telepathically warned her to *shut up*.

Without missing a beat, she changed the subject. "Okay, so what do we do now?"

Thank God, telepathy worked for once.

"Let's sleep on it," Megan said decisively and pushed off her car. "I had a rough week and it's nearly midnight. We can regroup in the morning. Maybe one of our sleeping brains will work out an answer."

I pulled out my car keys and glanced at my Civic, still in the parking spot where I'd left it when I escaped with Jax. In my mind I saw Tom Davis staking out my apartment, his grin evil as he watched me unlock the door. *"Hold it right there,"* I would hear behind me. Startled, I would whirl round, keys pushed outward between my fingers to use as a weapon. *"Stay back! I don't have the diamond!"* A harsh laugh would explode out of him. *"We'll see about that. You're coming with me."* He would knock the keys from my hand and clasp a chloroform-saturated cloth over my nose and mouth. My arms would flail helplessly as I sank into unconsciousness—

"I can't go home!" I burst out. "What if Tom Davis is waiting for me? It wouldn't take much effort for him to track down the address of the person who owns Flawless Paws. Me."

"Well, if you can't go home, neither can I!" Bree cried, stricken. She paced away several steps, then spun to face us. "We're roommates. He saw me at the shop, too. How will he know I'm not you? Did you tell him your name? No, you did not. What if he thinks I'm you? What if he beats me up? Rips off my fingernails? Drills holes in my teeth—"

I stared at her, aghast. I hadn't even thought of that stuff like that. My thoughts raced. A chloroform-saturated cloth was pressed against my nose and mouth, my arms flailed helplessly as I sank into unconsciousness, the ominous sound of a drill whirring in the background...

I pressed a hand to my chest. "Listen, Television Tammie," I said, trying to sound as though her words hadn't just catapulted me into panic mode. "No need to go over the top. Obviously neither of us can go home tonight."

"I'd say you could stay at my place, but no dogs allowed. We'd never get these big mutts past the guy at the front desk," Megan said.

"Wait. Why will we still have dogs?" Bree asked. "Petey will go home with Jax, and we can deliver the other two to their owners. Why keep them any longer?" She lifted a shoulder in a half shrug as if to emphasize how much of a no-brainer this was.

"It's too late to drop off the dogs. We'll give someone a coronary calling or banging on the front door so late. I can't afford to alienate customers." I rubbed my tired eyes so hard that tears squeezed out of the inner corners. I could almost hear my mother admonishing, *Don't rub your eyes, it'll break blood vessels.* I kicked at a stone and sent it flying across the parking lot.

Jax cleared his throat. "Maybe you could—"

"I suppose we could go to my parents," I said slowly, "but I'll have to be prepared to answer a bunch of questions about applying to vet school and the new guy I told them about, Colin." *I should never have lied in the first place.* "And we'll have to invent a good reason why we can't stay at our apartment and why we have these dogs." *Hmm. New lie needed.* "And just to be clear, we are not telling them about continental breakfast and what really happened because I don't feel like dealing with their reaction when they learn about the idiotic place I've landed in."

"It's not idiotic," Bree said. "You just hit a speed bump on the road to true love."

"All they'll see is, business as usual for me." I blew out a frustrated breath. "Maybe we should stay at one of those motels on the frontage road. They're cheap. And they probably won't care if we have a couple of dogs."

"You mean those places that, ah, rent by the hour?" Jax asked, blinking.

"How do you know about that?" Bree asked at the same time I said, "They're all not that bad. There's that one, Moonlight Serenade, with the picket fence. It looks kind of homey—"

"Busted last year, site of a major prostitution ring," Megan said. "Didn't you hear about it?"

"If I had, I wouldn't be recommending Moonlight Serenade now, would I?" I said crabbily. "Okay then, how about that other place about half a mile down."

Jax raised a hand. "Ladies, I—"

"The Bates Motel?" Megan cleared her throat.

"Very funny. I happen to have friends who stayed there and came out alive," I said.

Megan wagged a finger back and forth, a firm rejection of that option. "I'm not risking it. Haven't you seen the old lady who runs it?"

"No." *Really?* Could nothing ever be simple?

"Pay attention when you drive by. She stands outside the office door all day long and just watches the cars—left, right, left, right. I swear, it's all day long. She's probably the son dressed up like his mother..."

"Seriously?" I asked. "Are you really a lawyer...or do you just play one on TV?"

"I have a solution," Jax said firmly. "You can all stay at my place. It's not big or fancy, but I can guarantee Tom Davis won't find you there because he doesn't even know I'm involved."

Shocked, I smiled at Jax, met his eyes with mine to say *thank you* without actually speaking the words out loud.

After a stretch of silence, Megan asked, "Who are you, again? And why should we think it's a good idea to stay overnight at the home of a complete stranger?"

"Yeah," Bree said slowly. "You can just go home and forget this ever happened. Why do you care?"

"I don't think we need to worry," I said, prepared to make a sales pitch on Jax's behalf.

"That's okay. Fair question," Jax said. "I care because, hell, that's just what I do. I protect things—forests, animals, water, those quiet places you go in the woods to restore your inner peace." He leaned a hip against Megan's car. "You three got sucked into this trying to help out some guy who left behind his briefcase. I got sucked in when I went to pick up my dog." He opened his hands, palms up. "Seems like we're all in the same boat. I'm just trying to help."

I felt like hugging him.

"You could be a serial killer for all we know." Bree's brow furrowed. "And we could all be dead by morning."

"Oh, for God's sake," I began, but Jax interrupted, saying, "For all I know, you three are professional jewel thieves. And every minute I'm with you my life is in greater danger." He opened his hands, palm up. "Look, I've got a bedroom with a queen-size bed—and a living room with a couch. You can barricade yourselves in the bedroom if you want."

I gave Bree a nudge. "Come on you guys, I just went into the shop with him alone and I'm still alive. Nothing happened." I remembered our kiss and a heat crept up my cheeks. *Well, almost nothing.* Nothing they needed to know about yet, anyway.

"Or stay at Moonlight Serenade," Jax said matter-of-factly. "Your choice."

Bree pulled a face. "Did you see that television program where they exposed the hotel rooms to infrared light and all sorts of gross stains showed up on the bedspreads and stuff? You know, stains from—"

"So, Jax, where do you live?" Megan asked. "Because I'm thinking it sounds just about perfect."

Jax's living room was stretched to its limits with four adults and three dogs sprawled from one end to the other. Petey was on the tan sofa between Megan and Bree; the other two dogs were stretched out on the floor. Jax had his feet up in a brown leather recliner. And I was in the old wooden rocking chair that he said his grandmother and mother had used to rock their babies to sleep.

"Who wants a beer?" Jax went into the tiny kitchen.

"Any red wine?" Bree asked.

He turned in the doorway and shoved his hands into his front pockets. "Pinot Noir, Merlot, or Cabernet?"

"Seriously?"

He snorted. "No. Do you want a beer or not?"

Bree's face fell and I let out a laugh. "He's a guy, Bree, what are you thinking?"

I looked at him silhouetted in the doorway, the kitchen light outlining his broad shoulders and strong frame. The dark growth on his jaw and the set of his eyes made him seem dangerous in the dim light. Yet for all that, the smile on his lips made me feel safer than I'd felt since this whole thing began.

A sensation slid through me, desire, like a drip of rain

on a window gaining speed as it slips downward. Who was this man who had rescued me?

"Beers all around?" he asked as he passed out bottles of a craft brew I'd never heard of before. He raised his bottle in toast. "To dates, diamonds, and dogs. May that combination never again come to pass in our lives. Now...let's figure out how to fix this thing."

Two beers later, we were left staring gloomily at one another. After brainstorming nonstop, the only problem we'd solved was who was sleeping where. At Jax's insistence (which included him changing the sheets to win the argument), Bree and Megan agreed to take his bed, I got the couch, and Jax got the floor. We all protested him giving up his bed, but he refused to consider any other arrangements, contending that a self-inflating camping mat and sleeping bag were all he needed: "Keeps me comfy in the woods. It'll do just as well in the house."

Though my only camping experience was with the Girl Scouts—and we'd slept on cots with mattresses in big canvas tents on wooden platforms—all I could think of was lying next to Jax in a tent, the crickets lulling us to sleep at night and the birds waking us in the morning as they chirped welcome to the rising sun.

"My brain is aching. Goodnight everyone." Megan picked up the t-shirt Jax had given her to sleep in. "Maybe morning will bring new perspective. Jax, thanks for the bed and the safe house." She came over to give me a hug. "Don't worry, Allie, we'll find an answer."

"I'm going to bed, too." Bree patted me on the shoulder. "At least we have three dogs who'll bark if anyone comes prowling around. Which they won't," she hastily added, "because nobody knows we're here."

I watched them retreat into Jax's bedroom. "Someone dream a solution, will you please?"

Jax finished off his beer, then stood and stretched his lower back. "I'm going to take the dogs out before we turn in. Want to come along?" He lifted the leashes from a hook by the door, and all three sleeping dogs instantly awoke and jumped to their feet as though a whistle had sounded.

We headed out into a night that was still holding tight to the day's warmth. The high clouds had blown off, and the sky was solid with stars flickering like sparklers on the Fourth of July. A soft breeze sifted through the darkness, tiptoeing across my cheeks and tousling my hair. I exhaled slowly, happily, feeling safe and content—if only for a while.

The dogs were ecstatic to be outside, dashing back and forth across the sidewalk as they sniffed every tree, every bush, every leaf on the ground. Jax and I had to keep trading leashes with each other to prevent them from twisting into a knot.

Two blocks down, we passed my car, parked on the street in the only space I'd been able to find. The neighborhood, a combination of duplexes and single family homes, had been built in the era before most households had two cars. Now, parking was at a premium and the streets were always lined with cars.

"These dogs have way too much energy for so late." I stepped over a leash that was wrapped around my legs, and Jax took hold of my arm to steady me. He slid his hand down my forearm and twined his fingers with mine.

I slanted him a shy sideways look and thought, *I guess we could do this for a while.* After today's events, it felt so reassuring to have his hand around mine. I knew it didn't mean anything. Wasn't a commitment. Didn't involve introductions to family. We were just two friends holding hands, giving the dogs a little exercise late on a summer night.

But the stars were twinkling *love,* and the breeze was whispering *romance,* and I knew I should say something before it all got awkward. Unfortunately, the only thing that kept coming to mind was the kiss we'd shared earlier —and I wasn't going to make that a topic of discussion. I'm not a total moron.

Luckily for my sodden brain, Jax broke the silence. "So, you like dog grooming?"

"It's good." Blaghhh. I sounded like teenager on her first job interview. I groped for a more intelligent response. "I like it. Most of the time, anyway. I love animals."

"I can tell, just by watching you with them."

Flattery will get you everywhere, I thought. "I always thought I'd be a vet. But after graduating from college, I just couldn't imagine doing more school. The funny thing is, when it came time to apply to vet school, I wasn't sure if the dream was mine...or my parents'. I started to question what I wanted, where I was going. Ended up getting a job in a pet grooming shop, and a year later, I opened Flawless Paws."

Jax gave my hand a squeeze. "You'll be working a long time. It's always a good idea to do something you love. Or, at least enjoy."

"That's the thing," I said. "I'm happy, but sometimes I wonder if dog grooming is what I really want to do."

Jack looked at me curiously. "So maybe vet school after all? Or something else?"

"I don't know. Sometimes it's hard to know exactly what I want because my family can be...overbearing when they're convinced they have the right answer. They need to give me space to...it has to do with—"

Did I really want to tell him about being the baby of the family and what that meant? I exhaled. "It has to do with them needing to let me make my own decisions..." *Stop treating me like a baby.* I chewed at my lower lip, thinking. That's what it was about, right? Them treating me like a baby...

Jax stopped and pulled back on my hand. His jaw was tight, his eyes locked on something down the block. Fear tripped through me. I sent my gaze flying over the cars lining both sides of the street, past the driveways and the pockets of deep shadow and streetlight dim. Nothing seemed out of place. Nothing appeared alarming. "What's the matter?" I asked in a low voice.

He put a finger to his lips. "This is just wild speculation. But Davis may have found us." He pulled me and the dogs behind a tall, leafy hedge shielding someone's backyard from the street, then peered through the leafy branches.

My chest tightened. "You saw him?"

"No. But see that Explorer parked over there? By the streetlight?" He pointed at a black SUV halfway down block.

I pulled a branch lower so I could get a better view. "The one with *WASH ME* in the dust on the hatch?"

"Yeah. When I arrived at Flawless Paws to pick up Petey, there were only three cars in the lot. One was a black, older model Explorer with *WASH ME* in big letters on the back end. What are the odds?"

I let go of the branch and it snapped back into place, the sound so amplified by my anxiety it sounded like a tree crashing to the ground. My mind began to charge in every direction, like a rat caught in the walls of a building, running up one beam and down the next searching for escape. "It can't be him. It's impossible. How could he have found us?"

"I don't know."

"We have to get back to the house." My voice ratcheted up a whispered notch. "What if he goes after Bree and Megan?" I pictured Tom Davis breaking in on my sleeping friends, and Bree screaming, *"Not my fingernails, not my fingernails."*

"Slow down," Jax said quietly. "We got out of the parking lot at Flawless Paws before he was ever close enough to see my license plate. There's no way he has my address."

I bit my bottom lip and tried to believe him.

"Your car is parked more than two blocks from my place," Jax continued in a logical voice. "So even if Davis somehow found his way to the neighborhood, your car wouldn't show him where we are. Plus, I closed all the shades, so he's not going to spot any of us through the windows."

"But what if it is him? How did he get this close?" And then it hit me. I pulled my phone from my pocket. "Maybe he's tracking my phone," I said breathlessly. "My phone number was in the message I left Colin at the hotel."

"Is your GPS on?

"I only turn it on when I need it."

"I think GPS has to be on for tracking. Unless he's a cop, then they can get help from the phone company. But I don't think he's a cop. They wouldn't have screwed around sending a guy to ask for the briefcase—they would have just brought a search warrant." He broke off to peer through the bushes again. His lips pressed into a straight line.

"What's the matter?"

"I'm not sure. Maybe nothing. Stay here with the dogs. I'll be right back."

"Where are you going?" I immediately conjured up a picture of Tom Davis, murderer, prowling the dark city streets like Dr. Jekyll—or was it Mr. Hyde? My mind leapfrogged to zombies and vampires rising from the dead to wreak havoc after sunset.

I quickly rammed a wooden stake through the heart of that undead thought.

"I just want to check something out, a theory."

"About what?" Not wanting to be left alone, I grasped both his arms and looked directly into his eyes. Whoever says you don't notice details in a crisis is dead wrong. You notice them even more. "Tell me," I said to those beautiful eyes, those sculptured cheekbones, that curl of dark hair on his forehead, that thick stubble on his jaw, those kiss-able lips, those eyes, oh those eyes...details, details, details. I was seeing all of them.

"Allie." He cupped my cheek in his hand and I leaned into his palm, wishing that we were just two people out for a late night walk after a first date instead of two people unwittingly caught up in a crime...or two...or, really, maybe even more.

"Tell me your theory," I said. "This is my life we're talking about here."

"Okay, but don't freak out. I'm thinking...maybe there's a tracking device on your car."

ELEVEN

Don't freak out? My life had become a spy thriller and I wasn't supposed to freak out? "I don't think I heard you right," I said in a fast, whispery loud voice. "Just say that again, what you just said. Because if you said that...thing about tracking...then I think someone in this group might be going over the top and, for once, it's not me."

"I know it sounds absurd. I only know what I've read in books or seen in movies." He had the good sense to look a bit embarrassed. "But if that's his SUV, how else could he have found us? If the guy has any connections at all, it probably was easy for him to find out if one of the cars in the lot belonged to you—especially since there were only two there."

Exactly. Made perfect sense. I got it. And Jax wanted me to stay back here alone, behind a hedge in the dark, five cars away from the SUV belonging to the guy who might have killed Colin? No way. No friggin' way. "I'm coming with you."

He rolled his beautiful eyes. See? The danger was growing and I was still noticing details. "You're safer hidden back here than you are next to your own car."

I shook my head vehemently. "I'm sticking with you."

"Allie—"

"You don't get a vote."

He exhaled slowly. "Okay, fine, but stay alert and be ready to run in case we see Davis."

"I'm ready to run. Trust me, I'm so ready," I said, following him down the block. I tried to walk silently like we did at Girl Scout camp, creeping through the woods on the outside edge of our moccasined feet, rolling from heel to pinkie toe for maximum stealth, stepping gently over sticks and leaves on the trails—and only losing our concentration when we stopped to argue over whether a plant was poison ivy or not. Luckily, poison ivy would be a non-issue for Jax and me.

The dogs trotted quietly beside us, ears pricked up and alert as though they sensed our fear. Once we reached my car, Jax motioned downward with one hand. "Stay low so you're in the shadows," he said.

I sat cross-legged on the grass, my back against the car. The three dogs jockeyed for position on my lap and I fended them off using my forearms like a Kung Fu master. I may love dogs, but if Tom Davis showed up, I wanted a full range of motion available to me so I could move quickly—and a lap full of love dogs would definitely be an impediment.

Jax went to the driver's side, dropped to the ground, and scooched under the car on his back. "Son of a bitch!" he muttered.

My stomach leapt. I rolled onto my hands and knees and bent over the curb so fast I tweaked a muscle in my side. "Did you find something?"

"A rock stabbed my shoulder."

I sat up and massaged my side and checked the street in both directions. With Jax beneath the car, I was feeling pretty vulnerable. Maybe I should have stayed in that other yard like he suggested.

A light appeared under the car, and I knew Jax was using the flashlight on his phone. When he shut it off without saying anything, I rolled onto my hands and knees again and peered under the car. "What did you see?" I whispered.

The only reply was a series of mechanical clicks followed by three blazing flashes of light that practically pierced my vision. *Pictures.* He was taking pictures of something. I shot upright and blinked into the darkness. The only thing I could see was an afterimage of the car's underbody, a photo negative that was seared into my brain by the camera flash.

Great. Just great. Tom Davis could be coming down the block at me this very minute and I wouldn't even know because I'd been temporarily blinded. I turned in either direction, listening hard. Noises creaked around me—rustling sounded in nearby bushes, soft tapping came from up the block, and a rough sliding sound echoed down the street...a sliding sound like...the Mummy as he dragged his foot behind him, white bandages trailing in his wake.

Sucking in a breath, I pulled my imagination out of overdrive.

I heard Jax scoot out from under the car, and I scrambled to my feet, blinking rapidly to force my night vision back to normal.

"Let's get off the street." He took a couple of the leashes, and we moved deep into a nearby backyard.

Terrified anticipation was making my imagination run wild, but I refused to let myself draw any conclusions until I learned exactly what he'd been taking pictures of. Maybe he just wanted to show me a hole in the muffler that I should get fixed.

"There's a small, rectangular metal box attached to your gas tank. Magnetic. My guess is it's a tracking device," Jax said in a tight voice. He swiped open his phone and showed me the pictures he'd taken, then switched to the Internet and ran a search for images of tracking devices.

The online pictures were almost identical to the thing under my car. My stomach clenched. "That's what it is," I whispered.

"He probably put it there after we took off in my car."

"That has to be his Explorer. He's around here somewhere. Nearby." I threw an anxious glance over my shoulder.

"Allie, don't worry. He may have found your car, but he has no idea which house you're in. My place is safe."

The dogs began to prance around us as though our tense voices were dancing music. Petey made a whining/talking sound and Jax shushed him. "Come on, let's go," he said, taking my hand.

"So what did you do with it?" I asked. "The tracking device."

Jax led me across a row of backyards, weaving a path past hedges and sandboxes and plastic wading pools without answering. Finally he said, "Nothing. I left it there."

"What?" I stopped abruptly next to an old wooden climber, a swing set long abandoned by its children as they grew to adulthood. "Are you kidding? We need to put it on a truck going cross country." I took hold of the climber. It wobbled slightly, making me think of the passing of time and how little of it I might have left.

Jax came so close I could make out his features in the darkness. "Great short-term solution, but Davis will figure out pretty quick that we're onto him," he said. "As long as he doesn't know that we know about the device, we have the upper hand."

If we had the upper hand, why did I feel like it could be curtains for me any minute? "If we have the upper hand," I said. "Wouldn't this be a good time to call the police? I know I've been against it, but if we showed them the tracker on my car, and tell them about the diamond and Tom Davis—"

"Maybe. I thought the same thing. The problem is, everything we've got is circumstantial," Jax said. "Yeah, there's a tracker on your car. And yeah, there's an Explorer here with *WASH ME* on the hatch like the one that was in your parking lot. But we have no proof this one belongs to Davis—"

"The police can check the plates."

"And what if it's not Davis's car, just some guy who lives in the neighborhood? Or what if Davis isn't his real name and the police say, *This car belongs to a guy named John Smith—not Tom Davis.*" His eyes narrowed. "Do you think his name really is Tom Davis?"

"No," I said in a muted voice.

"Me neither. So, if we get the police out here, and they check the plates and tell us the car is registered to someone else—"

Disappointment coursed through me. "I'll lose credibility."

"Especially if you start talking about briefcases, diamonds, murder, and dogs."

"Not to mention continental breakfast." I slapped an open palm against the wooden climber. "They'll think I'm a crackpot."

"Which would be okay—"

"What?" I glared at him.

He chuckled. "Just kidding. The problem is, when we really need their help because we've got Tom Davis in our sights—"

"They'll think the crazy woman is at it again. They won't take me seriously."

"Right. So here's what we need to do—watch that SUV until the driver shows up. If it's Davis, we call the cops. Simple as that."

"And if it's not him?"

"I don't know. But we can't have someone arrested for having *WASH ME* on his car." Jax took my hand again and gave a tug. "Come on, we're wasting time."

We crossed the street, cut across a backyard in serious need of mowing, wove around some fences and garages and through an alley. The whole thing was beginning to feel like an out-of-body experience, like I was already dead and watching a rerun of the hours leading to my demise.

"It's almost one in the morning, and I'm skulking about in people's yards," I muttered. "How did my life morph into this? Diamonds, murder, thieves, tracking devices, fake names, bad guys—"

"Good guys," Jax said with a grin, and my heart melted.

"One good guy." I smiled back even though my stomach was knotted so tight it hurt. "I thought only the FBI and police could use tracking devices."

"Not anymore. Haven't you seen the commercials? *See where your kids are going with the car,*" he whispered like television announcer. He gestured with one hand, accidentally tugging back on the leashes around his wrist and causing the dogs to stop. "*Or follow a cheating spouse.*"

"So, thinking out loud here," I said in a low voice, as if I were being analytically philosophical when, in reality, I was getting more anxious by the second. "Why don't we use the tracker to draw Davis out? If I start driving my car, he'll follow. We'll be able to tell right away if it's him and can call the police. Just like that, it'll be over."

Jax shot me a patient look. "Great idea. Except what if Tom Davis isn't working alone, and the person who follows you is some guy in a second car? Or what if there's a third car that forces you off the road—"

"And they torture and kill me?" My voice went up four notches across six syllables. Whirring drills and chain saws sounded in my mind.

"Easy does it," Jax said, shaking his head. The standard poodle snuggled next to my legs as if sensing I needed comfort.

We cut through Jax's backyard, and he unlocked the side door. "Allie, we're not going to take any unnecessary risks," he said as we went inside. "We don't have to force Davis to tail you. All we have to do is find him. If he shows up at that Explorer, we call the police. Everything's done safely, *from a distance.*"

I unsnapped the leashes from the dogs' collars.

"Keep the shades closed and don't open the door unless it's me." Jax turned the lock to make sure it automatically latched when the door shut.

"Wait a minute, you're not going back alone." I caught the door before he could close it. "I thought we were just dropping the dogs off."

"It's too dangerous for you."

Even though I didn't want to be out there, I didn't want Jax out there alone even more. "But you need me. You don't even know what Tom Davis looks like," I protested.

"You know even less because of your memory wipe," he retorted. "I got enough of a view when he chased you across the parking lot."

Shit. What was I supposed to say to that? *Oh, heh heh, pay no attention to that memory wipe thing?* I'd already lied twice about the wipe—I couldn't come clean now. "What if he recognizes you? Or you need backup?"

Jax put a hand on each of my shoulders. His eyes locked with mine. Need I even mention my visceral response? Sigh. "He won't recognize me, and I won't need backup because all I'm going to do is sit in the bushes. If Davis shows, I'm calling the cops. That's it. I'm staying hidden until they arrive and arrest him. Then we'll all go down to the station to tell the story."

"I can hide with you."

"No." Jax stepped outside. "I'll text you as soon as it's over. I've got your number from when you called about keeping Petey overnight." He pulled the door shut, effectively ending the discussion.

I got what he was saying, but it didn't make being left behind any easier. Frustrated, I paced across the room a couple of times. Ran my hand over the books on his shelf without reading any titles. Dropped onto the couch to wait. Petey tried to climb from the floor into my lap and I held him off. He touched my leg with one paw and let out a low, drawn-out whimper.

Oh. My. God. I let out a huff. "Fine, come up here."

Big mistake. All three dogs took it as a personal invitation and immediately jumped onto the couch, flopping around on the cushions until they were comfortably squashing me between them in contented happiness. I might be feeling the love, sure, but I was also feeling the claustrophobia.

I slouched into the sofa and stared, unseeing, at the ceiling, hoping beyond hope that the Explorer belonged to Tom Davis and that he would be apprehended tonight. If he was Colin's killer and got away, I could hardly imagine what my life would be like going forward.

The big problem was, I knew what he looked like. And it would be in his own best interest to make sure I wasn't around to identify him someday. If he never got caught, I might always be in danger. I'd have to wear wigs and dress in disguise. Always be looking over my shoulder, never able to trust anyone for fear of betrayal. I might have to close my business. Maybe I'd have to go into the witness protection program, change my identity, move away, leave my friends and family.

Hmm. A definite upside; at least I wouldn't have to worry about finding a guy to impress my parents anymore.

On the downside, though, I would never be able to borrow Jen's awesome clothes again.

Just kidding. Of course I would miss my family—at least as much as Jen's clothes.

Just kidding again.

I picked up Time magazine from the coffee table and began to absently flip through the pages, my mind galloping. If I went into witness protection, who got to choose my new name? Surely, I would be able to give input. After all, what would be the point of sticking me with some name I hated, like *Miranda*?

I know Miranda isn't the worst name, but there was a mean girl in my fourth grade class named Miranda who would say things to me under her breath like, *"Allie Allie OXen Free."* You know, like *Olly Olly Oxen Free*, that thing you yell in Hide and Seek to get everyone to come out? She put special emphasis on *ox* because I still had some baby fat. My grandma used to say I was *sturdy,* but she meant it in a good way.

Anyway, one day I said to one of my friends, "I canna standa Miranda," and she repeated it to other kids. Pretty soon everyone was saying it, which made Miranda cry and made me feel like I was the mean girl instead of her. And I wasn't a mean girl—it was just a defensive maneuver. So anyway, my point is, I would rather not be reminded of all that every day of my life.

I always thought it would be cool to have a take-control name like *Kate*. People just naturally respect Kates. It's probably the hard letters, the K and the T, that make it so powerful. My full name is Allison, all vowels and soft letters, a name to wrap in a blanket and cuddle and boss around—no wonder my family still treats me like a baby.

I'd need a new no-nonsense last name too, with hard consonants, like...oh... I scrunched up my face thinking. Gardiner. No. Garner. No. Garrett. Hmm. "Garrett," I said aloud. Petey lifted his ears.

"You like it?" I asked. "Garrett. Kate Garrett." It had power. Like Bond. James Bond.

With a name like that, my life could be totally different. I could be running companies, corporations, maybe even countries... *"Good evening, Madam Secretary, the President is waiting for you,"* the security guard would say as I entered the White House for an emergency meeting. I would nod. *"Hello, Ronald."* I would greet all the guards by name because, as Secretary of State, I would be at the White House all the time. *"They're waiting for you in the President's office..."* Ronald would say, *"And Madam Secretary, may I just take a moment to thank you for all that you do to keep America and the world safe."* I would smile at him, touched that—

A rumbling growl from the golden retriever yanked me out of my daydream. The sleeping dog was curled into a tight ball, his legs twitching as he let out a few whimpers. Probably chasing a squirrel across the yard in dreamland. I let out a sigh, envious of his carefree existence.

Too wired to sit still any longer, I wandered into the kitchen to make some coffee because, you know, there's nothing like caffeine to settle your nerves. As soon as I was off the couch, the dogs stretched across the cushions to fill the space I'd vacated.

I worked my way through the cupboards until I found coffee cups and a bag of Starbucks coffee, then put enough scoops in the coffeemaker for half a pot. It had almost finished brewing when Megan appeared in the doorway wearing the big t-shirt Jax had lent her.

"What are you doing?" she asked, squinting.

"Making coffee. Want some?" I got out another mug and sent it on the counter.

She shuffled into the room and sat at the old wooden table. A moment later, Bree shuffled into the room, also wearing one of Jax's tees. "What's going on?" she mumbled. "Am I missing something?"

"Coffee," Megan and I said simultaneously.

Bree peered into the living room. "It's the middle of the night, for God's sake. Where's Jax?"

"That's why I'm making coffee." I lined up three mugs on the counter and filled each with the steaming brew as I filled the girls in on everything that had happened since they'd gone to bed. "We think Davis attached the device after the dogs and I escaped in Jax's car."

The lawyer in Megan kept her from showing much reaction, but Bree's eyes might have popped from their sockets if they'd been able to. "Whoa. A tracking device?" Bree held up both hands as if surrendering. "Did I travel to a parallel world in my sleep? Ohhh, wait. I'm dreaming, right? This is a dream." She laughed, a touch of hysteria in the sound. "You're all in my dream. Well, goodbye! Dreamland is closing. Time to wake up! Wake up!" She squeezed her lids shut, and then popped them open. Her brow furrowed. "What? Do I have to click my heels together, too?" She lowered herself into a chair at the table as if she wasn't quite sure what to believe.

"Not a dream," Megan said. "This is reality."

Bree turned to me for confirmation.

"Sorry. It's real. You have no idea how much I wish it was a dream." I set mugs of coffee in front of her and Megan.

"You know, the bearer of bad news gets beheaded," Bree said.

"Yes, well, for this bearer of bad news, that may turn out to be painfully close to what actually happens." I put a half gallon of milk and a couple of spoons on the table.

Bree poured some milk into her coffee. "All we wanted was to meet some guys. Really, just one guy for each of us—"

I slid into an empty chair. "Don't worry. We have a plan."

"Well, it better involve the police because..." She took a swallow of coffee, then quickly hoisted the half-gallon of milk to her mouth and drank from the container. "Aghh, I just burned my tongue. What I'm saying is, we're in over our head. *Or heads.* Maybe the problem is that even though we have three heads, we collectively have just one brain, because omigod, how did going out to continental breakfast get us in a place where there's a tracking device on your car and a potentially dangerous man on your tail?"

Closing her eyes, Bree inhaled deeply through her nose, exhaled through her mouth, and tapped her index fingers together as she hummed, *"Ohm."* After several seconds, she opened her eyes. "I just needed a moment of meditation. Okay, what's the plan?"

I gave my head a shake to clear away the free-flowing turbulence Bree had brought into the room. "Jax is doing surveillance from a backyard near the Explorer. If Tom Davis shows up, he's calling the police."

"That's the plan?" Bree gave me an incredulous look, one that said she was holding herself back from spouting something sarcastic like, *You must have spent hours working that one up.*

"Seriously Allie, is that it? Because...did you give any thought to the fact that the police can't be there in seconds?" Megan poured some milk into her coffee and gave it a quick stir. "If Tom Davis gets in his car and drives away, he'll be gone before the cops even leave the station."

I frowned at her.

"They can track the license plate. Jax got the number, didn't he?" Bree asked.

"I'm sure," I said, not sure at all. "Probably took a picture of it."

"If it's a stolen vehicle, the plate number won't help." Megan picked up her coffee cup. "He can dump the car a mile away, jump in a different car or take off on foot. Doesn't matter which, he's gone."

How could Jax and I have not thought of these things? How could the man who'd been so careful when we went back to search the shop have overlooked such important details?

"The only way this plan could work is if Jax detains Davis until the cops arrive," Megan pointed out.

That's when it hit me. Jax hadn't overlooked anything. He hadn't made any planning errors. He didn't want me out there because he knew he wasn't going to stay hidden. He was going to do whatever was necessary to keep Davis from getting away before the police arrived. I'd just been so tired and traumatized, I hadn't realized what he was up to.

"He refused to let me stay with him," I said.

Megan sipped her coffee. "He was protecting you."

"Nice guy," Bree said with a smile.

"Really nice guy," I said softly. Fear for him snaked through my belly.

Middle-of-the-night stillness settled over us as we drank our coffee and contemplated the situation in silence. After a minute, Bree set down her mug and sat up straight. "Four of us could definitely take down one man," she said.

TWELVE

"My thoughts exactly," Megan replied. "There's no reason Jax should be sitting alone in the dark, preparing to take on this guy alone."

Something caught in my throat and I swallowed hard. "Really? You two are possibly the best friends anyone could ever have." I concentrated on my mug. "It was one thing when I thought Jax would call the police from the safety of a hiding spot. But now...what if he confronts Davis and the guy pulls a gun?"

"I thought the gun was all in your imagination," Megan said.

"Yeah. But that doesn't mean he doesn't have one."

"We just have to be smart," Bree said. "Like I tell my students, hope for the best, but prepare for the worst. Take no unnecessary risks."

Megan swept a hand through the air. "Surprise and darkness will be our allies—"

"We'll be stealth," Bree added. "And armed." She gazed around the kitchen like she was doing an investigation. "There's got to be some stuff here that we can use as weapons."

"So? Do you want to do this?" Megan asked, her expression intense.

I thought of Jax out in the night, ready to take on Tom Davis by himself. "Absolutely."

Bree glanced at the clock on the stove, ticking toward one-thirty. "We got here hours ago. If Davis followed the tracker signal as we drove, that means he's been in the neighborhood for hours, too. At this point, he may be ready to call it a night."

Megan gulped her coffee and shoved back her chair. "We better get moving. Bree, let's get dressed. Allie, see if you can find some things we can use to stop him...a base-ball bat, rope, anything like that. Too bad we don't have any pepper spray."

She and Bree went into the bedroom, while I started whipping my way through the kitchen drawers. Tin foil, plastic wrap, dish towels, utensils, silverware, knives. I stopped. *Sharp knives.* As in butcher, steak, and paring. The thought of running down the street with one of those knives, let alone actually using it on a person, gave me the willies. I pushed the drawer shut.

I shifted my attention to the cupboards. Pots and pans,

plates, glassware, food, vinegar, maple syrup, olive oil. I reached for the can of cooking spray—pressurized canola oil. Hmm. A shot of cooking spray to the face might be as debilitating as pepper spray. Sure couldn't hurt to have along anyway. I put the can on the table, added a frying pan for good measure, and hurried to the back hall closet.

Tugging the door open, I surveyed the contents. Nothing seemed promising. A few jackets and hooded sweatshirts dangled sloppily from hangers, a plastic grocery bag over-filled with plastic grocery bags was spilling onto the floor, running shoes, hiking boots, a fire extinguisher still in the box, and a vacuum cleaner. Too bad the fire extinguisher was so unwieldy because it had real potential. I patted the vacuum thoughtfully, then removed two of the hard plastic extension tubes, twisted them together and slapped them against my open palm. "Yeeow." I rubbed my stinging hand on the front of my jeans. "That could...inflict damage."

I took a bungee cord off a hook and stretched it between both hands, then put it back. I wasn't going to be dumb enough to try to tie someone up with elastic binding. I reached up to dig around on the shelf. Four baseball caps, a winter scarf and gloves, ski mittens, some sort of balled-up netting, and a bike helmet. As I pulled the netting down, it unrolled to the floor, and I discovered it was an old hammock with rope tied to each end for attaching to trees. The hammock wouldn't be useful, but the ropes might come in handy if we needed to tie Davis up. My stomach lurched at the thought, and I started to work at one of the tight knots.

"Any luck?"

I jumped about a foot and glared at Megan.

"Sorry," she said. "What'd you find?"

"Take your pick." I gestured at the stuff on the table and handed her the club I'd made out of vacuum extension tubes. "I found some rope on this hammock, just need to get it untied."

"I grabbed a belt from the bedroom." Bree came down the hall. "I can use it like a whip."

"Oh, I've got a big picture of that," I muttered.

"You don't think I can do it?"

"You think you can and that's all that matters." Megan picked up the frying pan from the table, then set it down again.

Doubts about what we were doing began to seep into my mind, and I pushed them away.

"What's the cooking spray for?" Bree asked.

"Poor man's pepper spray."

"Nice." Bree picked it up and struck a defensive pose, legs apart for balance, one hand holding the belt, the other holding the can of cooking spray straight-arm in front of her. "En garde," she said as she snapped Jax's belt against the chair back.

Oh yeah, we were ready for anything.

Megan slapped the vacuum tubes against the palm of her hand a couple of times. "Let's go. We need to get there before Davis does." She strode across the living room. "Allie, bring the hammock. We'll untie the ropes once we find Jax."

She pushed open the front door, and the dogs tried to follow her outside. I waggled a stern finger at them. "You're not coming along. If you three had behaved in the first place, we wouldn't be in this mess."

Once outside, I began to retrace the route Jax and I had taken to get home. "We'll be harder to spot if we stay off the sidewalk," I said. Though the night was darker than before, I didn't switch on my phone's flashlight. Why risk having homeowners call the police because of a strange light moving through their backyard?

I started out confidently, weaving around some hedges and past a couple of fences. After a few minutes, I stopped beside a white garage to reset my bearings. Where was the alley Jax and I had followed? More importantly, *how does one lose an alley?* I started to change direction, then stopped again. Garages and trees and bushes all loomed dark, wrapped in impenetrable shadows as though hiding the undead. I shivered.

Something skittered through the grass, and I stumbled backward, clutching the hammock protectively against my chest. "I thought we came this way," I said, peering at the ground to make sure that thing, whatever it was, didn't run across my feet. "But I'm sort of turned around."

Navigation has never been my strong suit—some might say I'm directionally-challenged. Give me a paper map, and I'm in trouble. I actually have to rotate it so it faces the direction I'm going, and even then, I sometimes get confused. All of which explains why I tend to make liberal use of the GPS on my phone.

"Let's go out to the sidewalk and see if that helps." Megan led us over some low bushes and across two backyards.

Once we reached the corner, I quickly recognized where we were. "Okay, I've got my bearings. Somehow I angled us left." I pointed down the block. "We just have to cross this street and the Explorer is at the end of the next block. Near it is a backyard with a tall hedge—that's where I think Jax is."

"First things first. Let's make sure the Explorer is still there." Megan bent low and ran into the front yard of a nearby house until she was hidden among the shadows and overgrown bushes.

As Bree and I crept stealthily after her, I felt a little like Darkwing Duck, cartoon crime fighter extraordinaire. "Let's get dangerous," I whispered in tribute to my child-hood hero. Hopefully, we would be as successful as he'd always been. And, fingers crossed that we wouldn't end up as bruised as he did in the process.

Half a block up, a man came out from between two houses and headed away from us down the middle of the street. Megan waved a hand behind her back, and we dropped to our knees—one, two, three—behind a row of forsythia bushes heavy with yellow blossoms. Though my stomach was roiling with nerves, the scent triggered a volley of random thoughts...summer vacation, hide-and-seek, kick-the-can, romance, kissing Jax...

Kissing Jax? *Good God.* There was absolutely no connection between forsythias and kissing Jax—except in my addled brain.

"Is that Davis?" Megan whispered.

I peered into the darkness, and held off replying until he passed under a streetlight. "Maybe. Who else would be out and about in the middle of the night?"

"It's the weekend. Lots of people are out late."

"Bree, what do you think?" I asked.

She watched the retreating man. "I don't know," she finally said. "It's dark, he's almost a block away, and we can only see his back."

The man stopped beside a dark vehicle—SUV or mini-van, it was hard to tell from this distance—but didn't open the door.

"Is that the Explorer?" Megan asked, her attention riveted on the unfolding scene.

I squinted, hoping it would help me see better. "It's in the right area. But I need to be closer."

"All SUVs look the same to me," Bree whispered.

Exactly. Although at least I was smart enough not to say it out loud.

"If that's Tom Davis, we can't risk him getting away." Megan stood, and I knew an executive decision was in the making. "Bree call 9-1-1."

If that really was Tom Davis, we needed the ropes off the hammock *right now.*

As Bree dialed, I anxiously tugged at the knots that apparently kept this hammock swinging securely through rain, snow, sleet and hail. Kind of like the post-man. Unfortunately, like the postman, those knots weren't giving up easily. They'd probably been tied so long, the only way to get them off would involve cutting them.

And we'd left all the knives at home.

"Yes," I heard Bree say into her phone. "There's an assault in progress." She launched into a description of the alleged assailant and gave our location. My mouth dropped open. *Breaking into briefcases...and now lying to a 9-1-1 operator?*

"No, I don't want to stay on the line," Bree said. "I need to help my friend before it's too late." She swiped off the phone and grinned at me. *"What?"*

"You lied to 9-1-1? I think you can go to jail for that," I said, working at the knot.

"I didn't lie. There'll be an assault under way by the time they get here."

"And if we don't hurry, he's going to get away." Megan gestured down the street.

I jerked my head up to see him standing next to the open driver's door of the SUV—and another man walking toward him.

"Jax," I breathed. "That's Jax!"

"That means the other guy is Davis. We need to move," Megan said.

"I don't have the ropes loose yet." I held up the hammock. "All we have is cooking spray, a vacuum tube... and a belt."

"Whip," Bree said.

Whatever.

Bree took the hammock from me and let it unroll to the ground. "We don't need the ropes. We can use this like a net. While Megan is whacking him with the tube, we'll throw this over him like he's a giant mackerel."

At least it was an improvement over snapping a belt at him.

And we had nothing to lose. If we didn't catch Tom Davis tonight, I might have to spend the rest of my days running scared because, on some dark night when I least expected it, he might decide to step back into my life. It could be the end of the line for me, *the last haircut*, as we dog groomers like to say.

Actually, I just made that up.

I suppressed a shudder.

Bree passed me the can of cooking spray. Then she and I took hold of opposite ends of the hammock.

"Okay, as quietly as possible, on the count of three." Megan gripped the vacuum tube in her fist like a club. We got off our knees and into a crouch.

"One...two...three...go."

Bent forward at the waist, Bree and I took off side-by-side, the hammock dangling between us. We ran slowly and silently through the dewy grass and onto the sidewalk, hidden by the cars lined along the curb like rows of Great Danes curled in sleep. That visual barrier kept the two men from spotting us until we were almost upon them.

As we sprinted into the street, Bree and I separated, stretching the hammock between us like fisherwomen ready to cast our net upon the sea.

"Aeeeeaaahhhhhh," Bree screamed like a wild karate master, her free hand cracking the belt out in front of her like a bullwhip.

"Yeehaaaaaaa," I screeched next to her, as I thrust the can of cooking spray in front of me like a rapier.

Davis's head snapped up and his expression perfectly telegraphed his first thought: *Invasion of the Zombie Women.* He started to run, but as a middle-aged guy carrying extra weight he couldn't move all that fast. We were upon him before he got more than a few steps away.

Bree and I hoisted the hammock over his head and shoulders as Megan smacked him with the vacuum tube. He grunted and tried to fend us off, but his fingers caught in the netting. I sprayed his face with canola oil. Bree whipped his legs with the belt. Megan hit him with the vacuum tube—until the top half flew off and clattered away in the street.

While she chased after the tube, Bree and I raced around Davis like children round the maypole, wrapping the hammock tight around his torso until he lost his balance and fell to the ground. Then Megan returned and stood over the guy, brandishing her reassembled vacuum tube like a broadsword.

I caught sight of Jax, incredulously shaking his head like he couldn't decide whether to thank us or read us the riot act. That was when the reality of what we had done sank in—we had taken down Tom Davis. My arms started to tremble, my muscles slackened, and the can of cooking spray slipped from my fingers and rolled into the gutter.

Wriggling like a worm in a cocoon, Davis demanded, "Let me out of here! What do you want?"

"Shut up. The cops are on their way," Megan said.

"The cops? Good. You'll be under arrest for assault," Davis snapped.

"And you'll be under arrest for theft and murder," Bree shot back.

"Are you people crazy?" Davis tried to wiggle free.

Jax steered me away from the group. "You okay?"

I opened my mouth intending to say, *It's the middle of the night and nothing feels real,* but what came out was, "I have to buy you a new can of cooking spray."

He laughed. "Hardly. I can't believe you girls did this. What if something had gone wrong? This guy could have been dangerous."

"That's why we did it. Because we realized you were planning to confront him—alone." My eyes blurred with exhausted tears. "Which was way more dangerous." I touched his arm. "Jax, you just met me. How do you think I would feel if something happened to you because you were trying to help me, almost a complete stranger?"

He half-smiled. "I'm not a total idiot, you know. I called the police before I went after him."

Sirens wailed in the distance, and I hoped they were headed in our direction. "We called them, too."

"Watching the cavalry come rolling in was pretty incredible." Jax ran his thumb down my cheek and over my bottom lip. "You three were something else. Especially you, but then I may be a little biased." His mouth curved up. "Ingenious use of my old hammock, by the way. And vacuum cleaner parts."

"Group brainstorming." I smiled back.

The sirens were screaming now, shattering the air just up the street. I knew I should be feeling a great sense of relief, but as the police got closer, my apprehension grew. What if they didn't believe us? What if they let Tom Davis go? What if his associates, the ones who wanted to buy the diamond, later got involved because they thought I was lying about losing the ring—and were convinced I'd actually stolen it? What if a rumor went out on the street that I had a big diamond—and every petty thief from here to Timbuktu decided to come after it?

Don't get me wrong, I was glad we'd apprehended Davis, but with the diamond still missing, catching him might not provide the total closure I wanted.

Two squads screeched to a halt a couple of houses down, sirens cutting off mid-squeal and leaving a lingering echo in my ears. Almost like magic, a spectacle began. Up and down the block, lights flicked on, pleated shades rolled open, people peered from between the slats of their blinds, and a few of the especially brave—or especially nosy, depending on your point of view—stepped outside to get a better view of the action.

Four officers jumped out of the squad cars. Megan met them halfway to the scene of the crime and managed to get in a few words about stolen diamonds and dogs before they reached Tom Davis. An older cop, graying at the temples, aimed a flashlight beam on Davis, while two others helped him to his feet.

"What is this?" one of them asked, unwrapping the netting.

"A hammock," Bree said proudly.

For some reason, I wanted to cringe.

The cop passed the hammock to Megan, then flashed a light on Davis. Cooking spray glistened across his thick cheeks and dark brows.

"Rob?" the older cop asked. "What's all over your face?"

Rob?

The cop's gaze slid to the four of us. "What's going on here?"

His authoritative tone triggered an outpouring of words from Bree, Megan, Jax, and me: "...after a diamond... wants to kill the dogs...just wanted to meet some nice guys...seemed like he was legit... Tom Davis showed up... chased Allie across the lot...didn't steal his diamond...just trying to reach Colin...threatened to kill Allie...a misunderstanding...all the good guys are taken...needed weapons...poor man's pepper spray..."

And in the middle of all that, Tom Davis pointed at me and bellowed, "That woman is a jewel thief. And she's fencing stolen jewelry."

Everyone froze for a split second, not just those of us in the street, but every person in the neighborhood who had stepped outside to watch the show. The atmosphere was like a volcano erupting, with voices ramped even higher and louder than before as all four of us began disputing Tom Davis's words, and he furiously double-downed on his accusation.

"Quiet!" The older cop shouted over all of us. He waved his hands. "Everyone shut up!"

So we did.

Megan gestured at Tom Davis. "Officer, I'm an attorney. Do you know this man?"

"Yeah. Rob Cramer. Private investigator."

What the hell? *What. The. Hell?* I looked at Davis/Cramer and tried to make sense of this new twist. "If that's who he really is, then you don't know enough about him. He said his name was Tom Davis," I burst out. "He's a liar and a thief and he's dangerous. He's trying to steal a diamond ring that belongs to...a guy I went out with. He was willing to kill three dogs to get it."

Davis/Cramer pointed a finger at me. "The real thief is

that woman. She has the diamond. She and her friends assaulted me. I want to press charges."

"You can't charge us," Bree said. "We're pressing charges against you—"

"Okay, okay, everybody shut up," the cop said. "Either I can arrest all of you right now and charge you with disorderly conduct, or we can all go down the station and have a nice chat and figure out what's going on. Your choice." He pulled a handkerchief out of his back pocket and handed it to Tom Davis. I mean, Rob Cramer. "Here. Wipe off your face."

Half an hour later, we were all seated around a large oval table in the conference room at the police station. A different cop—Officer Wickham—had taken over, names had been exchanged, and coffee had been distributed in white Styrofoam cups.

It turned out that Officer Wickham knew Davis/Cramer, too. All the cops did; he'd been a private investigator in the area for years. Somehow I knew this was not a point in our favor. At that moment, I felt kind of like a batter at home plate—ninth inning, two outs. I could almost hear the announcer's voice: *A swing and a miss. Strike one.*

"Thank you all for coming down here for this... meeting of the minds," Officer Wickham said from the head of the table. "Let me make clear that since you're all here voluntarily, you're free to leave whenever you want. No one is under arrest."

Not yet anyway. He was nuts if he didn't think we were all finishing that sentence in our minds.

The officer nodded at Cramer. "Rob, why don't you go first?"

I threw a worried look at Megan. Obviously, everything he said was going to prejudice the police against me. *Strike Two,* the announcer in my brain whispered.

This whole thing was crazy—and unnecessary. If Cramer had just come clean with me in the first place, maybe we could have worked together instead of against one another. Maybe this wouldn't have become such a traumatic life experience. And maybe we wouldn't all be in the police station right now talking about disorderly conduct and pressing charges.

"I'm working on a case that has a confidentiality agreement." Cramer rested his left hand on the table; the four gold rings on his fingers shone like freshly polished brass knuckles. "So I can't give you my client's name. But here's the basics."

He clasped his hand together like an altar boy and directed his words at the officer. "I got a call from a woman whose grandson stole some of her jewelry and sold it for drug money. Necklaces and bracelets. A diamond ring. He's young, been in trouble before. Family's got him in rehab now. She didn't want the police involved, didn't want publicity, just wanted her stuff back—but only if it could be done quietly."

He sat back and took a slurp of coffee, his left eyebrow still glistening with cooking spray. "If it wasn't possible to do it quietly, she was going to let the whole thing go. Family reputation and all that. She'd rather lose the jewelry than risk her grandson getting a record or sent to juvie. Anyway, during my investigation, Colin Hughes's name came up—"

"Because he runs the Intercontinental Jewelry Exchange?" I asked hopefully. Please, please, I begged the universe, don't let me be such a bad judge of character that I thought a crook was my ideal man.

"No, because he's a thief and a fence." He smirked as though he thought I was feigning ignorance about what Colin really did.

I thought of the charming man I'd met for breakfast and drinks. He wasn't a successful businessman, didn't run an international company, wasn't a multi-millionaire. I'd been so thrilled with how impressed my family would be, I ignored the warning signs. I'd believed everything he told me because I *wanted* it all to be true—not a very adult response, I had to admit.

It was small consolation that I'd never actually introduced him to my family. Even though they didn't know the truth about Colin, I did. I knew I had screwed up again. Rather badly.

As though reading my mind, Jax caught my eye and

winked to boost me up.

"I tailed Hughes Thursday morning," Rob Cramer was saying. "My plan was to—*retrieve*—the jewelry in the least dangerous manner possible. Avoid confrontation. So I followed him to breakfast at Tucker Point Hotel and saw her—" He jabbed a finger in my direction. "—meet with him there."

THIRTEEN

My jaw dropped. Tom Davis, I mean Rob Cramer, had been at continental breakfast? I tried to remember seeing him, but he wasn't in the age range or looks categories I'd been targeting. Probably because I'd skipped right over him on the way to Dashingly Dangerous iPhone man or Clean Cut and Classic New York Times man.

A nervous, high-pitched laugh slipped out of me. "I can explain." I waved a hand as though the whole thing was really no big deal. "You're correct, I did make contact with Colin. But I went there to—" *Oh, just wait until I said this out loud.* "I went there, of course, to eat breakfast, and... not to meet Colin, but to meet—"

"Please. Let's hear Cramer out," Officer Wickham said.

Rob Cramer rubbed a lump on his forehead that was already blooming purple. I winced. The damage we'd inflicted would do nothing to endear us to him or the police. His fingers slipped across his canola oil brow, and his attitude hardened. He wiped his hand on his pants. "Later that night," he said, "I followed Hughes to Sullivan's restaurant where he passed off his briefcase to Ms. Parker. That's when I knew something very valuable was changing hands—probably the jewelry I was trying to retrieve."

He was at Sullivan's, too? Had he seen me eat two full platters of Irish brown bread and goat cheese?

"Oh, oh, oh," I said waving both hands now, my voice rising with emotion. "I can explain this so easily. We were on a date! But then Colin had to return an urgent call and couldn't get phone reception, so he went outside—"

A thought buzzed into my brain, went round and round like a bee pulling a banner, the message whipping past again and again until it finally sunk in: what if Colin had noticed Rob Cramer at breakfast and then spotted him again at Sullivan's? What if—w*hat if he thought Rob Cramer was a cop on his tail?*

Colin had been distracted that night—twitchy and nervous. He kept looking away from, and then he left in a rush and never came back. I leveled my gaze on Cramer. "Were you sitting in the back at Sullivan's? By the bar?"

"Yeah. So what?"

"Ahh!" I choked out. Suddenly, it was all making sense. "Colin kept looking back there. He tried to hide it, but I could tell something wasn't right. I thought maybe he wasn't used to dating. But what if it wasn't that at all? What if he saw you at breakfast and then again at Sullivan's? He would have thought you were following him—*that you were a cop.*"

I pressed my palms together for emphasis. "Don't you see? Colin didn't leave the briefcase because he was passing off the jewelry. He left the briefcase because he didn't want to get caught with that jewelry in his possession!" I had never been so proud of my powers of deduction in my life.

"Do you write novels?" Cramer asked dryly.

Jax cleared his throat and addressed Officer Wickham. "Whatever Colin's reason for leaving the briefcase, the bottom line is, Allie only took it to keep it safe."

I bobbed my head to affirm his words. "I was Colin's date—not his contact. Who could possibly mistake me for a diamond fence—" I broke off as another thought rammed its way forward. What if Colin had been expecting to meet someone at breakfast, someone interested in buying stolen jewelry...and I showed up at his table first? What if Colin thought I was his contact?

I scrolled back through all our conversations, from the first meet to the moment he left the restaurant, every weird, awkward sentence. Oh. My. God. It couldn't be true —could it?

That's when I knew there was no other reasonable explanation for everything that had occurred. Obviously, Colin met with me both times expecting to sell stolen jewelry. But I'd been so determined to meet an eligible man, I put everything he said through a romantic filter—

and ignored all the warning signs that something wasn't right.

"This whole thing is about mistaken identities!" I announced. "I mistook Colin for an eligible bachelor. When I approached him at breakfast, he mistook me for his contact. Then, Colin mistook Rob for a cop. Don't you see? It's just a series of misunderstandings." I smiled triumphantly at Officer Wickham, certain that everything would soon be over.

After a long beat, he said to Cramer, "Can you speed this up?"

Did he not believe me? Maybe I hadn't been clear enough. I opened my mouth to repeat my epiphany, but Cramer beat me to the talking.

"Like I said before," he said, "I avoid confrontation. Decided I would follow Ms. Parker until she left the brief-case in her car or at home and I had an opportunity to *retrieve it.*"

"You mean steal it?" Bree's voice was unnaturally high.

"The jewelry was *stolen* from my client. I would merely be getting it back for the rightful owner." Cramer gave a careless shrug. "Anyhow, while I was in the restaurant I got a phone call. The signal in Sullivan's was so bad—"

"See?" Bree clapped twice. "That proves what Allie said about Colin's phone!"

Officer Wickham glared at her.

"I went to the window to get a better signal," Cramer said, ignoring Bree. "Coincidentally, that's when Ms.

Parker took off. Like she was waiting for me to get distracted—"

"I didn't even know you were there!"

"When I turned around, she was escaping out the main door with her arms wrapped around the briefcase like she knew exactly what it contained. By the time I got outside, she'd disappeared. Must have had a getaway car."

Escaped? In a getaway car? "Hardly," I said with as much indignation as I could muster. "I had a great parking spot right around the corner, that's all. *Nothing illegal.*"

I nodded at the officer hoping to get him to nod along, and thus, be more inclined to side with me, but he didn't move. Instead, he scribbled some notes on his pad of paper. "So how'd you find Ms. Parker again?" he asked.

"I went back to the hotel to ask some questions about Colin. The front desk gave me the message she'd left for him—about having the briefcase at a dog grooming shop."

Megan held up a finger. "If Colin purposely gave the briefcase to Allie, why would she leave that message? Why would she try to give the case back?" she said in her best *you-have-no-case* voice.

Officer Wickham rubbed his jaw. "Criminals aren't always the brightest lights on the tree. Maybe returning the briefcase is how they exchange the money."

"Bawwaaaaa," I said, because somehow I sounded guilty even to myself.

"Ms. Parker, please control yourself," he said, and I knew I was fast losing credibility.

I took a big swallow of lukewarm coffee to shut myself up.

Cramer then described how he'd gone to Flawless Paws, and how I'd given him the briefcase because he said he was a colleague of Colin Hughes and how the case contained all the jewelry that his client was missing. Except a diamond ring worth half a million dollars.

At least it wasn't worth a full million like Bree thought, but it was still a very valuable bauble...one that I couldn't find.

"I had a hunch she lifted it from the case and was going to sell it herself. So I went back to Flawless Paws to confront her," Cramer continued in a smug voice, "and that's when she told me a dog ate it."

"Actually, what she said was that one of three dogs ate it and she wasn't sure which one," Bree chimed in.

Officer Wickham's mouth tightened into a straight line, and I suspected Bree wasn't helping the cause.

"Right," Cramer said, "Told me she'd call when the ring was...out. At that point, I didn't know what to believe. Didn't know who was working with who, who was selling, who was buying. But if she was telling the truth, I knew the fastest way to find the diamond would be to have the dogs scanned—"

"That is *so* not what he said." I gripped my Styrofoam coffee cup. "He said there are faster ways to get a diamond out of a dog—"

"Which meant an X-ray." Cramer rolled his eyes like I was some kind of crazy.

"But when he said it, he had a look...almost a murderous expression. I felt threatened. Like the dogs and I were in grave danger. So I took the dogs and ran out the back door."

"That's when I came into the story," Jax said. "He chased her out of the building—"

"And with good reason," Cramer snapped. "She had possession of a diamond that didn't belong to her—and was refusing to give it up." He went on to explain that once Jax and I escaped, he'd run license plate checks on the two cars left in the parking lot to see if one was mine. Then he'd stuck a tracking device on my gas tank and tracked the car to Jax's neighborhood—where he'd come into contact with me and my friends. And the cooking spray. And the hammock. And the vacuum cleaner tubes. He rubbed the egg on his forehead again. It had doubled in size since we got there and was now several glorious shades of green, blue and purple.

Officer Wickham gave me his attention. "Okay, your turn," he said in a bored voice.

That's when I knew that no matter what I said, this inquisition was not going my way. Wickham was already convinced I was a member of Colin's diamond fencing ring —and we hadn't even gotten to Colin's death yet. Wait until that nugget got thrown in the mix. Wait until the police discovered I was with Colin the night before he died. It would be the smallest of leaps for them to conclude I killed Colin so I could keep all the jewelry without paying for it. And that I'd left the message at the hotel to throw the cops off my trail.

Stee-rike three. Batter's out, the announcer intoned in my brain.

A shudder flew up my spine and wrapped its fingers around my throat. My breath caught, and I forced myself to exhale and inhale and exhale. I needed to get out of that room. I needed to get out immediately. No more talking. No more waiting to get charged. Just escape and figure the rest out later.

"Miss Parker? Allie?" Officer Wickham looked at me expectantly. "You can tell your side now."

I gave him my sweetest, most apologetic smile. "Is it all right if I use the restroom first? All this coffee..."

"Go ahead. You're not in custody. Down the hall on the left."

As I hurried for the door, Bree jumped to her feet. "I have to go, too."

Damn. I didn't need her along to complicate things. I tried to discourage her with a frown, but she was oblivious. Side-by-side, we walked down the hall, not speaking until we got into the ladies room, all white and gray tiles like an old hospital bathroom. After using the facilities, we met at the sinks.

"How do you think it's going?" Bree asked.

I took an appraisal of myself in the mirror. My lids

were drooping from fatigue, my mascara was smudged, my hair needed to be combed, there was cooking spray on my shirt. Overall, I looked like hell. Which was a far cry from my impeccable appearance at continental breakfast last Thursday morning. "About as good as I look."

"Just explain exactly what happened. He has to believe the truth." Bree ran the water until it was warm, then washed her hands.

"Sorry, he's already accepted an alternate version of the truth. I don't think there's a word I can say that he'll believe. And we haven't even gotten to Colin's murder yet." I moistened a paper towel and wiped the smudged mascara from under my eyes. "He knows Rob Cramer personally. They've all known him for years. To them, I'm just some lunatic *doggg groooomer*. I'm in a hole so deep even pole vaulting wouldn't get me out."

Bree bent to splash water on her face. "It's not that bad."

"You go ahead and think that. It's not your future hanging in the balance. It's mine. And I'm not waiting around to get charged with theft, possession of stolen goods, and murder." I dragged the elastic band off my ponytail, used my fingers to comb through the scraggly mess, then pulled my hair back and twisted the band round it again.

Bree straightened; water ran down her cheeks and dripped onto her shirt. She pulled some paper towel from the dispenser and patted her face dry. "What are you talking about?"

"I'm talking about *The Fugitive*."

"Are you crazy?"

"Crazy like a fox."

"No, no you're not. You're exhausted and not thinking straight," Bree said, beginning to freak. "Allie, you can't go on the run. This is insane."

"What's *insane* is for me to stay here. I'm getting out, getting lawyered up, and then I'll talk to the police." I knew I was sounding a little whacked but I didn't care. I had just spent the last forty hours being buffeted by a series of events that had escalated beyond my control. I was done being tossed about—I was taking charge of my life. I walked over to the window.

Bree grasped my arm. "Allie, no! That won't solve anything!"

"I'm just investigating options." I pulled away from her. "Bree, I haven't been arrested. I haven't been charged. We're all free to go—Officer Wickham said it right in the beginning."

As I went for the door, Bree jumped in front of me. "Okay, okay," she said. "So just tell him you're leaving. It's the considerate thing to do."

I snorted out a laugh. "Right. And that's when I'll be arrested. I'm not going down for a diamond ring I didn't steal or a murder I didn't commit. Better that I disappear now, find some legal advice, and have my lawyers get in touch later." I waved a hand at the toilet stalls. "Just say you were in a stall when I left. That you had no clue I didn't go back to the conference room."

Bree shook her head. "It won't work. You have to go through the main lobby to get out."

"Which is why I'm going down the hall the other way. There has to be a back door."

"Allie—"

"Are you with me or against me? Are you going to help send an innocent woman to jail?" I knew I wasn't playing fair. After twelve years of Catholic school, Bree had tons of guilt. She always struggled with gray area questions like: if a family is starving, is it a sin for the father to steal a loaf of bread to feed his children? And by extrapolation: If he refuses to steal a loaf of bread that would save his children's lives (because it's a sin) and instead lets them die, is he without sin? We've actually had this discussion and I'm happy to say that she agreed the father should steal the loaf of bread.

Bree let out a long sigh and I knew she was thinking about the starving children and the loaf of bread. "It's too open out there. Even if you go the other way, they'll see you. Let me go out first and create a distraction."

"No. You stay out of it. This is my problem—I don't want you to get in trouble."

"I was there when we lost the diamond, I'm probably already in trouble." Her lips curved down. "Also, before we go any further with any of this, I just need to say... I don't think anyone needs to know about Phinneas."

A lie of omission. Bree had just taken two giant steps into solid gray area. My conscience started to prick at me, but I pushed it away. Our intentions had always been pure. We'd never meant to do anything wrong, things just kept happening. "I agree. We were just fiddling with the locks on the briefcase and happened upon the right combination."

Bree threw me a quick smile. "Okay, then. Are you ready? Because I'm going out to...do my thing."

"Thanks, Bree. I owe you."

"No, you don't. We're friends. This is what friends do. Especially for friends who are being railroaded...or whatever it is that's happening here." She pushed through the restroom door and I caught it just before it closed, held it open a crack so I would be able to tell when to make my move.

Half a minute later, I heard Bree say, "Excuse me. Excuse me. You, and you, too. And you over there." She was talking in her firm, you-kids-are-in-big-trouble teacher's voice. "Who is responsible for the coffee around here?"

No one answered. Undoubtedly, everyone was shocked silent. I grinned.

"The coffee you brought into the conference room is awful," Bree said.

I heard a couple of people laugh. "It's always awful," a man said.

"That's just unacceptable." Bree's voice went up a notch. "I cannot believe we expect the men and women who protect the public, *with their lives I might add*, to drink that swamp mud."

Swamp mud? It didn't seem that bad to me, but the cops must have thought so because there was a low murmur of assent.

"Do you have any of that flavored creamer to mask the taste?" Bree asked. "French vanilla? Irish cream?" Another pause. "None? Well, put that on your supplies list. And FYI, the liquid creamer is so much better than powdered."

Silence ruled for a moment, and I could picture Bree making eye contact with everyone in the room to ensure she had their full attention. "Creamer, however, is just a bandage," she declared. "Let me show you the secret to making an excellent cup of coffee using a drip coffee maker and canned coffee. Gather round."

I knew they were obeying because, well, not only is Bree good at controlling a group (come on, she teaches high school) but if you were drinking swamp mud on a daily basis, wouldn't you want to learn how to make better coffee?

As I heard Bree saying, "The first step is very, very cold water," I slipped out the door and hurried down the corridor in the opposite direction, mentally sending her a thank you and a hug. There had to be another way out. Public buildings never had just one door.

The hall came to a T, and I spun right and then left. A red exit sign gleamed at the end of the corridor and I strode toward it, passing closed doors on both sides, offices with windows that overlooked the hall, all of them dark at this late hour—except one. Light poured from the window, brightly illuminating a section of hallway.

I slowed my pace and considered my options. Okay, my *option.* I really only had one: keep going. *Walk on by.*

I tried not to think about the fact that I was on the run. Which, technically, I wasn't, because I hadn't been arrested. Or even detained. I was simply taking control of my life. Like Richard Kimble.

Hopefully, proving my innocence wouldn't be as hard for me as it had been for him. Because there was no way I would ever jump off a two-hundred foot dam into raging water like he did.

Act like you belong, and you belong. It had worked at continental breakfast; might as well give it a try at the police station. I set my shoulders and strode forward, vowing not to glance into the window as I passed by. Despite my resolve, my eyes slid to the right on their own, desperate to make sure the room's occupant wasn't noticing me.

Not to worry. The guy was dozing in a chair behind a small conference table, his head slouched to one side. He almost looked like—

I stopped. *Fuck.* "Colin?" I whispered. My thoughts began to career inside my skull, bouncing off the sides, banging into one another screaming, *He's not dead! He's not dead! He's not dead!*

Wait. Wait. Just wait. Was that really Colin or was I just seeing what I wanted to see? I pressed my face close to the glass. It sure looked like him—well, a messy, dirty version of him. I checked both directions down the hall, then reached for the door handle and tried to twist it open. Locked. *Damn.* Raising a fist, I rapped crisply on the window with my knuckles. I needed answers and I needed them quickly.

The man cracked open his eyes, then sat bolt upright. His hair was sticking up and he obviously needed a shower, but it definitely was Colin. And he was not happy to see me.

I pointed at the doorknob and motioned for him to open it. Scowling, he mouthed, "Locked."

He couldn't get out and I couldn't get in. "What happened," I mouthed back.

He shrugged.

Really? That was the answer he was going to give me after disappearing from Sullivan's and then showing up on TV, dead? I glanced down the hall again, afraid Officer Wickham would have the whole force searching for me any minute.

"Why are you here?" I mouthed.

He shook his head and irritably waved me away. Twice.

What was going on? When Rob Cramer said he'd been following Colin Hughes to get the stolen jewelry back, none of the cops even acknowledged his name. Yet, they already had him in custody. Why wouldn't they say something?

I let out a laugh. Who cared? It was all secondary. What mattered was that Colin wasn't dead. I didn't need to get an attorney. I didn't need to become a fugitive. I felt buoyant, like if I took a deep breath I might float to the ceiling. *Colin was alive*. He could confirm my entire story—or at least enough of it to put me in the clear. I pivoted on the spot and practically skipped back to the conference room.

"Allie!" Bree's mouth opened and closed like she couldn't decide what to say.

"Went the wrong way." I gave a self-deprecating grin. "Directionally challenged. Got lost in the corridors."

"We were starting to wonder," Officer Wickham said. "Okay, so you want to explain your side of the story?"

I slid into my seat, confident beyond measure. "Yes, absolutely, I will. In full-spectrum color detail. In a minute. But first I want you to know that—*I know Colin Hughes is alive*."

Megan and Bree gasped. I threw them a confident smile. "That's right. He's in an office down the hall." I focused on Officer Wickham. "Don't even try denying it. I saw him, alive and well. No way is anyone pinning his murder on me."

FOURTEEN

"Who said Colin Hughes was dead?" Cramer asked.

"What do you mean, he's down the hall?" Officer Wickham interrupted. "Are you saying a member of the police force is a jewel thief?

I blinked, my thoughts scattered with confusion. "Breaking News said he was dead." My mind jumped back to the news story I'd seen on the television in the bar. Closed captioning scrolling along the bottom of the screen said a man had been pulled from the river. But, the part about him being dead...well, I hadn't actually seen that. Bree put it in her text.

"I saw it on TV," I said slowly. "And Bree did, too, on a different channel." I turned to her for backup. "You sent a text that he was dead. That was on the news, right?"

She winced in slow motion. "I didn't see the whole

report. Megan and I were at happy hour and I just happened to look at the TV."

I had a premonition that what she was going to say next wasn't what I needed to hear. My body started to overheat.

"I saw Colin's picture on the screen just as the report ended," Bree said. "So I asked a guy at the bar what it was about. I just texted you what he told me."

After a pause, Megan said, "Apparently he didn't see the whole thing either."

I was so simultaneously relieved and mortified, I couldn't even speak. Colin had never been dead. Not one second. I'd been running around like a maniac thinking I would be charged with murder for absolutely no reason.

Jax set his elbows on the table and leaned forward. Eyelids drooping, middle-of-the-night tired, dark stubble on his jaw...and all I wanted to do was keep looking at him. "What the hell is going on?" he asked. "Why is Colin Hughes in an office down the hall?"

Officer Wickham's jaw tightened. "I need to know who you're talking about—" He pointed at Rob Cramer. "Can you I.D. Colin Hughes?"

"Absolutely."

"I can, too." Bree stood. "I saw him at continental breakfast."

"Two will be enough." The cop motioned to me. "Okay, show us this guy."

I led them to the room Colin was in, then stood back

and waited. Cramer stared in the window so long, I was afraid he was going to say it was someone else. And if that happened, I had no idea what to do next—maybe make a mad dash for the stairwell.

"That's him," he finally said.

My knees almost gave out from relief.

"He's not a cop," Wickham bit out. He didn't say another word until we were back in the conference room.

I was jittery with anticipation and the cautious hope that, maybe, just maybe, everything would get cleared up and I could go back to life as usual—grooming dogs, going out with my friends, complaining that I couldn't meet a guy, having my parents bug me about going to vet school... you know, all those happy moments I loved.

Officer Wickham thrust a hand through his thinning hair and pressed his lips together as though debating how much information to share. "Some teenagers hanging out on the riverbank saw him hit the water. Called 9-1-1. As we were fishing him out, the kids took a picture on a phone and sent it to a couple of television tip lines. Thought they'd get a reward or something."

He pushed back in his chair. "Colin Hughes wasn't the name he gave us. I won't tell you what he said his name was, but we ran a search on it and got no matches. No driver's license, no criminal history. He also wouldn't say how he ended up in the river—suicide, mugging, a fight—just wouldn't talk. So, standard procedure, we put him in that room and decided to search for some answers before interviewing him again."

I rubbed my sandpaper dry eyes. "None of this had to happen. If Colin had been a halfway decent communicator, this would have ended at continental breakfast. All he had to do was ask how much I wanted to pay for the jewelry, and we both would have realized I was the wrong person."

"That's irrelevant now." Cramer settled his gaze on me. "We're here because you stole my client's ring. And because you and your friends assaulted me."

"And because you were threatening and stalking Allie," Bree cried.

Apparently, just because I was cleared of murder didn't mean all my problems were going away.

Officer Wickham gave a snort. "Okay, everyone, let's get back to the reason we're having this...little gathering. Ms. Parker, want to tell your side of the story? Quickly, if you can?"

So I told the whole convoluted story in the most straightforward manner possible, including all the very intelligent and logical reasons why we went to continental breakfast in the first place. I noticed Officer Wickham's lips twitching more than once, but I appreciated that he never actually laughed out loud.

When I finished, Jax said in a very reasonable voice, "Obviously, this is a case of mishaps and mistaken identities. Allie thought Colin was a potential...boyfriend. He thought she wanted to buy stolen jewelry. Mr. Cramer thought the two of them were working together. As a result of that belief, Mr. Cramer's behavior—including stalking —made the girls think their lives, and the dogs' lives, were in danger." He steepled his fingers. "The girls had a valid reason to be afraid of him—"

"And it appears to me he violated some laws along the way," Megan added.

Officer Wickham looked at Cramer. "They make a good point, Rob. You want to charge them with assault, they may want to charge you with stalking, what with that tracking device and all. Know what I mean?"

Cramer scowled at me. "Just give me my client's ring and we'll call it a day."

"I told you," I said quietly, trying to keep my fears at bay, "we can't find it."

"We've searched the place twice," Megan said.

"I was there when it happened." Bree added. "It's gone. Disappeared."

Cramer's face reddened. "You know what this looks like?" He pointed an accusing finger at me. "They stole the diamond from Colin and now they're trying to keep it."

"That's not true." Megan sat up ramrod straight, ready to do battle.

She was an awesome person to have on your side. But this time, it wasn't going to matter. From the beginning, I knew we were going to end up here—Cramer would insist on getting the ring back and I didn't have it to give. Stalemate.

"Please. I promise you we don't have the diamond." My voice quivered despite my efforts to hide my distress, and tears filled my eyes. "I would give anything to hand it over to you and go back to grooming dogs for the rest of my life."

I couldn't believe I had become the stereotypical female weeping in a disaster. Do men cry in moments of stress? No. Well, maybe some do. But then they pull it together and fight back.

Get mad. Be a guy, my brain urged. So I brushed off my eyes, sat up straight, and met Cramer's glare with one of my own. "I know it's hard to believe. I can hardly believe it myself." I forced my voice to stay level. "Maybe it rolled into a crack and under the floor. Maybe another dog found it later and swallowed it. We've searched and searched—but we can't find it. And if we can't find it, we can't give it to you."

And then, even though I was being the best *guy* I knew how to be, much to my own chagrin, all the stress I'd been holding in for the past forty-some hours let loose and I began to sob. So much for overcoming female stereotypes.

"I didn't steal the diamond, I don't want to go to jail." I swiped the side of my hand across my nose. So classy. "All I wanted to do was meet a nice guy to take to my parents' forty-fifth anniversary so they would quit treating me like a baby."

Yes, I could totally see the irony of me blubbering like a baby while professing my wish to no longer be treated like one. But in my defense, it was the middle of the night, I was practically delirious from lack of sleep, and I was pretty sure there was no way to fix this disaster.

Officer Wickham gazed up at the ceiling like I'd made such a spectacle of myself he wanted to give me a few moments to pull myself together. Bree held out a tissue. I wiped my eyes and nose as I drew several calming breaths.

After a minute, Wickham said in a thoughtful voice, "As I consider the different aspects of this case from both sides, I'm struck by the fact that, other than Colin fencing stolen jewelry, we don't seem to have a lot of crimes here. Yes, Ms. Parker took possession of stolen goods—*the jewelry*—but it's obvious she didn't know it was stolen. And when the person she thought was the rightful owner showed up to retrieve it, she willingly handed it over. Would you both agree?"

"Yes." I held my breath, hoping Rob Cramer didn't bring up my recitation of *The Highwayman* to show that I hadn't actually been all that willing.

"Yes," he said grudgingly.

I exhaled.

"Next, we have an allegation about a stolen diamond ring," Officer Wickham continued. "But no one has filed a report about a stolen ring—or any stolen jewelry, for that matter. *Not one complaint has been filed.* Rob did you want to file a report about a stolen ring?"

"You know I don't—my client doesn't want publicity."

Wickham shrugged. "So, as far as I know, this ring—that no one has in their possession—isn't missing either. I'm not sure how I charge someone with stealing a ring that isn't missing." He took a drink of what had to be cold coffee and grimaced. "Finally, we've got the alleged diamond fence, Colin Hughes, in custody, but we've got nothing on him. He has no stolen jewelry in his possession. And if, when we question him again, he denies knowledge of the briefcase or the jewelry—which is what a smart thief would do—he walks."

He looked around the table. "I'm not seeing a lot of legs here. I'll tell you all what. Rob, you forget about your assault and theft charges—you've got no case anyway—and ladies, you forget about your stalking charge. You all do that, and I won't charge any of you with disorderly conduct and disturbing the peace. Have we got a deal?"

Everyone nodded. And with that, it was over. Leave it to the police to change what had been a mountain, a few hours ago, into a molehill.

Officer Wickham had someone drive all of us back to Jax's neighborhood so we could get our cars and go home. No one spoke during the ride, but once we got out of the squad car, I apologized to Rob Cramer again, took his card, and promised about twenty times to call if the diamond ring ever showed up. As I waited for him to retrieve his tracking device from my gas tank, Bree jumped into the passenger side of Megan's car. They pulled away from the curb before I could point out that it made more sense for Bree to ride with me since the two of us were roommates.

"See you later," Bree shouted from the passenger window, grinning ear-to-ear and giving me two thumbs up. She knew exactly what she was doing...leaving me alone with Jax.

Cramer hoisted himself to his feet, dusted off his pants, and plodded wearily down the street toward his SUV. Despite everything that had happened, I felt bad for him. He probably wouldn't get full payment for the job because he couldn't find that diamond.

That damn half-million dollar diamond. It was so far outside my reality, I could hardly fathom it. I watched Cramer drive away, the words scrawled in the dust on his hatch almost glowing under the streetlight. "Think he's on his way to the car wash?" I joked.

Jax nodded distractedly, the type of response someone gives when his mind is a hundred miles away and he's not even hearing you. He tapped his bottom lip with one finger, and I half expected him to come out with something like, "The sum of the squares of the two shorter sides of a right triangle is equal to the sum of the square of the longest side." You know, like the scarecrow when he gets his brain.

Instead he said, "My mom had a pet turtle when she was a kid."

Not quite $E = mc^2$.

"A baby one," he continued. "Back when it was still

legal to buy pet turtles." He held his thumb and index finger about two inches apart. "She let it crawl around on the floor at her grandma's and it disappeared."

It was the middle of the night and he was going to start musing down memory lane on the back of a turtle? Clearly, he needed some sleep.

"I just have to get the dogs from your apartment and I'll get going." I pulled out my car keys.

Jax ignored me. "Turned out, it fell down the cold air return. So they went into the basement and opened this door on the furnace. There it was, still alive, covered in dust."

I was pretty sure he wasn't talking about a turtle anymore. "What's a cold air return?" I asked. Everything I knew about machinery I learned on a need-to-know basis. Furnaces were a perfect example of that philosophy at work; the sum total of my knowledge about furnaces was that they created heat.

"It's a..." Jax paused. I could tell he was searching for a way to make his explanation simple. "It's a grate in the wall or the floor, connected to ductwork. Works like this. Hot air comes out of the room's vents and pushes the existing air into the cold air return. The cold air goes to the furnace, gets reheated, and sent back up to the vents."

"A circle of heat," I said, slightly embarrassed that, until that moment, I hadn't understood how the system worked. Although in my defense, my apartment has radiators and not vents, so clearly it's a different method.

"Anyway," Jax said. "I don't remember seeing a cold air return in your back room. Do you?"

I shook my head. "In the main room there are two that are probably cold air returns. I never knew what they were for because no heat or air conditioning ever came out of them. But the back room?" I scrunched up my face.

"Let's go take a look." Jax's eyes sparkled.

I appreciated his enthusiasm, but I was coming down from almost two days of non-stop adrenaline and nearly twenty-four hours without sleep and I wasn't feeling very optimistic. "Jax, I'm really tired. And the ring would have had to fly through the doorway between the two rooms and around a corner to even get close to a cold air return. It's not possible. Besides, I still have two dogs in your apartment."

"We'll take the dogs with us so you can go right home afterward. He grabbed my hand and began to run toward his apartment. "Humor me. I've got a feeling about this."

Jax ran a hand across the metal grid cold air return on the wall in the main room of the shop.

"No way could that ring have flown all the way over here," I said somewhat peevishly. "It's too far."

"Yeah, I agree." Jax went into the back room, flipped on the light, and began to slowly walk the room.

"And there's no cold air return in here," I said. "I would have seen one."

"Oh, ye of little faith. What's that?" He pointed at the lower row of cages.

"What?" I followed the line of his arm. "Where?"

He crouched down. "Lower. Behind the middle cage, half covered."

I peered into the shadows. "Sorry, but I don't see anything."

Jax flipped on his phone flashlight and directed the beam into the cage. "There," he said. "See it now?"

Maybe lack of sleep was making him hallucinate. I could hardly blame him; I was almost ready to collapse myself. Just as I was about to suggest we come back in the daytime, Jax shifted the flashlight angle and, in the changed light, I spotted what he was talking about—a metal grid on the wall behind the cage, its cross pieces in nearly perfect alignment with those of the cage.

I sucked in a breath, feeling more than a bit ignorant. "Oh my God, that's a cold air return. I never noticed it before."

"Why would you? It's at the back of a kennel in the bottom row."

"Not to mention the lighting. It's really dim back here. And the kennel usually has a big dog in it," I added to make myself sound less unobservant than I apparently was.

Jax grinned at me. "Exactly." He sat back on his

haunches and looked around. "So, let's go see if a half-million dollar diamond ring is like two-dollar turtle. Where's the door to the basement?"

I blanched. He wanted to go into the basement? Oh shit. No way. There was a reason I thought of *Attack of the Zombie Women* when Bree, Megan, and I were charging at Tom Davis, I mean Rob Cramer. It's because I went into the basement of my shop once.

Once. That's all it took.

It's the sort of basement where, in the movies, everybody knows zombies are living there, but they go downstairs anyway. And then they're stunned and terrified when they're attacked and turned into zombies themselves. Duh.

A zombie apocalypse ending would be par for the course with the way my life had gone the past few days. I considered suggesting we wait until the sun came up, but I didn't actually know if zombies were afraid of daylight. Vampires definitely, but zombie rules seemed to change from movie to movie. It probably depended on how they became zombies in the first place, whether through a virus, a mutant vaccine, a zombie bite...

"Allie? Something the matter?"

I gave a start. No way was I going to say any of that to Jax. Just because my imagination liked to create wild scenarios, didn't mean I was oblivious to how ridiculous those scenarios would sound out loud. I heaved a sigh. "You lead."

I handed him the flashlight from my desk and reluctantly followed him down the worn wooden steps. The lone lightbulb dangling from the cracked ceiling at the top of the stairs, cast a harsh, yellow light on the stained stairwell walls. It was low-budget, B-horror movie all the way.

With each downward step, I could feel the zombie presence grow.

I was traumatized by the undead way too young. Growing up, my siblings let me stay up late to watch vampire and werewolf movies with them and their friends when they had to babysit me. They were college students home for the summer, and I was an impressionable first-grader. It's their fault I can't come up the basement stairs without picturing monsters chasing me. Even now, I still charge up the steps two-at-a-time.

As we neared the bottom of the stairwell, I pictured us crossing the basement to the room where the furnace and hot water heater were housed. *"Be careful, Jax,"* I would warn. *"There may be something else inside that room. This basement... I can feel it, can smell it...undead. Just be careful."* Jax would peer uncertainly at the furnace room, then back at me. As the door began to open on its own, Jax would catch my hand and pull me up the stairs. We'd slam and lock the door at the top and he would thank me for warning him as I gasped to catch my breath, while whispering, *"Zombies, zombies live here—"*

"Zombies?" Jax was looking at me over his shoulder.

Omigod, I had to quit letting my mind get away from

me. I let out an overly exuberant laugh. "This basement just creeps me out. Make me think of monster movies."

"Not to worry. I'm a slayer."

"I should be so lucky," I muttered.

We stepped off the bottom stair into the cool, damp basement, and I tugged the pull string to switch on the bare lightbulb at the ceiling. Its dull glow illuminated just enough of the room to send my pulse racing and shoot my *fight or flight* response into overdrive. Okay, what actually happened is that *fight* went into hiding and only *flight* actually kicked into gear.

The walls were dirty and cracked, with chunks of concrete missing as though something had tried to claw its way out of the basement. A stain of water trickled down one wall, becoming a thin rivulet crawling across the floor to escape in the floor drain. And the air, ugh. It was heavy with a musty odor that some people might attribute to mildew, but others might describe as the smell of undead flesh.

Omigod, I had to stop this.

I told my brain to knock it off, that there were no such things as zombies and vampires. "The furnace is in that room over there." I pointed across the basement at the wood wall that someone had built a century ago, its yellow paint now faded and peeling. "Behind that door."

Jax seemed totally unfazed by the ambience—or lack thereof—and headed directly toward the room. I hesitated a moment, then followed him, walking sideways so I could keep my eyes glued on the darkness at the other side of the decrepit basement...to make sure we didn't get jumped by, well, God knows what.

I sighed. Some fears are just impossible to overcome.

Jax opened the furnace room door, and pulled the string to switch on the light. "Nobody here but us humans," he said.

I let out the breath I'd been holding.

He knelt on the dirty concrete floor next to the ancient metal furnace and pulled open the access door. The hinges shrieked like something half alive and tortured, and I let out an unnerved squeak that caused him to startle and smack his head on the furnace. "Fuck, Allie."

"Sorry," I murmured, chagrined.

He handed me the flashlight, then pulled out the furnace air filter and set it on the floor. I aimed the light into the space behind where the air filter had been.

Jax grunted. "It's loaded with dust back there. Probably a hundred years' worth of grunge." He made a sound of disgust. "Better get a garbage bag because we'll need to empty this out."

I sprinted upstairs and returned a minute later, chased all the way up and back by a host of imagined demons. "I brought two." I spread one plastic bag out on the floor. "We can sift through the dust on top of this one, then dispose of it in the other. To make sure we don't miss the ring."

Jax reached into the furnace with both hands, scooped up a thick pile of dark gray dust, and spread it across the plastic bag. We dug around in the filthy mess until we were sure the ring wasn't there, transferred the debris to the second bag, and repeated the process again and again and again—each time getting the same results. Nothing. Finally, Jax pulled something out of the dust and brushed it off. "Look at this."

My heart skipped an expectant beat and I moved closer to see what he'd found.

He held up a small plastic army man. "Imagine the stories this guy could tell. The people it's seen. The secrets it holds."

Yeah, like zombies. From the last century.

He set the soldier off to one side and went back to the furnace to bring out another pile of dust and dirt that, again, delivered nothing. The dim light, the dampness, the musty odor, and my imagination combined to send a shiver of foreboding through me. I stood slowly, fear prickling my spine as I stared into the darkness on the far side of the sprawling basement. Maybe we were on a wild goose chase and the longer we stayed down there, the more at risk—

"Hey Allie."

Startled, I spun back to Jax. He was on his knees facing me. "I know we only just met," he said getting up onto one knee, a broad grin splitting his face and brightening his eyes. "But...will you...marry me?" He held out his hand and even before I aimed the flashlight's beam, I knew he'd found the ring.

"Yes!" I pumped my hands into the air and let out a whoop, then dropped to my knees to throw my arms around him. "Yes!" I shouted. "I mean, no! No! Even though you're brilliant—" I planted a happy peck on his cheek.

"And amazing," he said.

"Absolutely amazing," I said, beginning to stand.

"And handsome," he said, preventing me from pulling away.

"Handsome," I repeated, smiling.

"Funny," he said.

I laughed giddily. "And funny."

"And irresistible," he said as he pulled me closer and I couldn't believe this guy was going to kiss me again, *that he wanted to kiss me again*, but it sure seemed a real possibility.

"Irresistible," I murmured. Oh, God, he was irresistible and I didn't know what to do about it. So when his mouth closed over mine, I did what every woman does when she's in a dark, scary basement full of hidden zombies getting ready to attack—I kissed him back.

FIFTEEN

THE SUN HAD RISEN WHILE WE WERE INSIDE THE SHOP, AND as Jax and I walked out the doors it felt like months had passed since this whole thing began—instead of just two days. I have to admit that with the discovery of the diamond—okay, and that second kiss from Jax—my exhaustion had fled and there was a spring in my step.

It was over, truly over. I could give Rob Cramer the diamond. I could tell the police I'd found the ring and given it back—if they even cared since no one had reported it missing. I wouldn't have to spend my life praying that, somehow, word wasn't spreading throughout the criminal underworld that I had stashed a half-million dollar diamond somewhere. Which meant, I would never have to go into witness protection. Not that I ever really thought that would happen.

The sun was shining. Life was good. I'd met an

awesome guy. It was Saturday morning, still the weekend. No problems on the horizon. Really, could it get any better than this?

And then my phone rang. I fished it out of my purse to see who could be calling so early on a Saturday. *Mom.* Who else?

What could be so important so early? Surely, Grandma wasn't in the hospital—no one would ever give me that information in real time. I only learned bad news after the fact. On the other hand, maybe right now was already after the fact, and mom was going to tell me that Grandma was safely recovered and had already been discharged.

God, it was hard to live this way.

"My mom," I said to Jax before answering the phone.

"Mom, it's six in the morning," I said as Jax and I headed for our cars, parked side-by-side in the lot.

"Oh, honey, I'm sorry to call so early. I just can't sleep late anymore. This will only take a minute. I just wanted you to know that Dad and I were talking and he said he will absolutely give the dean of the vet school a call if you want him to."

"*Mom.* I already said I didn't want him to."

"I know, but these days it's not what you know, it's *who you know.* Your dad is in a position to be able to help, so why not let him?"

I stopped walking, speechless.

"Allie?" my mom asked. When I didn't reply, she launched into a story about Jen's five-year-old's T-ball game, and how my niece had been playing first base but she was more interested in the dirt on the ground than in tagging anyone out.

That was my mom's usual strategy when she knew she'd overstepped; defuse the situation by changing the subject to something innocuous. As she talked, I let my gaze slide up to meet Jax's and gave an apologetic shrug.

We reached our cars: Jax unlocked his door, I unlocked mine, and my mom blabbed on. Jax smiled at me across the hood, and I realized that, quite possibly, I could never get enough of looking at those blue eyes and that dark, messy hair, and—

"...and just wondering, are you seeing that new friend this weekend?" my mom asked.

"What new friend?" I asked distractedly, smiling back at Jax.

"The one you told Jen about—"

Colin. Shit. "Oh yeah, I saw him," I said. *Being interviewed at the police station.* Good thing I'd never told my parents his last name or they would already have conducted an Internet search and discovered he'd been pulled out of the river. And then my dad would have talked to his contacts at the police station and learned at least some of what was going on and, oh God, they'd be all disappointed in me again.

"Dad and I are going out to breakfast this morning," Mom said. A new place that just opened. Do you want to join us? We could talk about vet school if you want."

"Breakfast?" I asked stupidly. Breakfast was what got me into this mess in the first place.

As she started to describe the restaurant and its menu, something deep in my brain—a brain fully accustomed to its position as baby of the family—shifted into a new place. It began to dawn on me that the more I let my family go down this well-worn path, the more they would go down it. They treated me like the baby because, oh hell, I was acting like the baby—making up guys I was dating, telling lies about vet school, not standing up for myself to my family members.

Even when I decided to become a dog groomer, I never shut down the dream—their dream—that I would become a veterinarian. I let their doubts about dog grooming take root in my mind, sometimes even entertaining the thought that maybe I should do something else when, in reality, I was really happy having my own business and being a groomer.

It had always seemed easier not to push back too hard. Easier in some respects...and if I was honest with myself, ultimately, harder.

That's when it dawned on me. What I wanted was my parents to respect me *as an adult*—and I'd never get that from them unless I started to act like I deserved it.

Jax climbed into his car and started his engine, and I knew I had to get off the phone with my mother and say something—anything—to him because he was going to leave and I didn't want to let this guy get away—

A call waiting beep sounded in my ear. Come on, another call so early on a Saturday morning? My life was beginning to feel like Grand Central Station. I pulled the phone away from my ear to check the number, but it wasn't one that I recognized. "Hold on, Mom, I've got another call," I said, and swiped to the new caller.

"Speaking of breakfast..." Jax's voice slid into my ear, and zizz shot through me.

I couldn't contain the grin that popped onto my face. "Yes?"

"I know a great place. Waffles, bagels, cereal, fresh fruit, coffee. All you can eat," he said. "Want to join me?"

I let out a laugh. "Hold that thought. I'll be right back." I put him on hold and went back to my mother.

"Mom, I'll make this quick," I said. "I'm not going to vet school and I'm sorry I brought it up again. That dream has always been your dream—not mine. And it's over. As for Colin...he was just a guy I thought you and Dad would like. But I've discovered something the past couple of days —he really isn't the kind of guy that I would like."

I began to walk across the parking lot so Jax couldn't overhear what I was about to say and misunderstand my reasons for saying it. "Mom, I'm happy doing what I do. Believe it or not, I feel fulfilled running my own business and grooming pets."

I glanced back at the forest ranger sitting behind the wheel of his car, tapping the steering wheel along to what-ever song was playing on the radio. "And the guy I end up with will probably be someone who...doesn't stay in five-star hotels and doesn't make a ton of money and doesn't discuss futures and puts and shorts and other financial things like he was born to it."

I thought about how Jax came back to help me even when he knew his dog was in the clear and he owed me nothing. "I don't care what the guy I end up with does. What I care about is that he'll stand by me when, as you always say, the going gets tough—"

"That's when the tough get going," she said quietly.

"Right. So, Mom, there's five months until Thanksgiving, and I want to tell you right now. I don't want to sit at the kids' table unless I choose to sit at the kids' table. Okay?"

"Okay."

"And how's Gramma doing?"

"Fine, fine. Dad just picked her up and took her home—"

I stopped walking. *They had pulled this on me again?* "She was in the hospital?" I practically screeched.

"No, no, she went on that bus tour to Yellowstone with the Senior Club. I thought you knew."

Right. Right, I did. "Oh yeah, sorry. Well, the next time anything goes wrong with her, I want to know as soon as it happens—not after the hospital discharges her."

"Okay." Mom's voice had gotten really small.

"And don't you or Dad ever tell me to floss again."

"Do we do that?" she asked as though she couldn't quite believe it.

I rolled my eyes. "Yes. Well, Dad does. You remind me to wear sunscreen—"

"Honey, I just don't want you to age prematurely."

I snorted out a laugh. "Well, I appreciate your concern, but I'll take my chances. Let me handle it from here on out."

"Anything else?" she asked sounding chagrined.

"Sure, but we can talk more later. I've got to go—I've got an important call on hold."

I swiped back to Jax as I hurried toward my car. "Are you still there?"

"Still here," he answered. "So...are you up for breakfast?"

"Maybe," I said coyly. "But, for some reason, all-you-can-eat doesn't appeal to me anymore."

"Not continental?"

"Definitely not continental." I slid into my car and started the engine. The dogs in the back seat perked up, ready for another adventure.

"Okay, because I know a great little diner, just a counter and two tables, but they serve the best over-easy eggs you'll ever have in your life. Up for it?"

"You're on," I said.

"Follow me." He shut off his phone and peeled out of the parking lot like he was at the racetrack.

"Anywhere you want to go." I put the pedal to the floor.

EPILOGUE

So, I gave the diamond back to Rob Cramer who almost passed out from shock when I showed up at his office with that sparkling turnip in a zip-lock bag. I told him all about the turtle and the cold air return and, like everyone who heard the story, he couldn't believe it.

He was so happy he insisted on taking all of us out to a Mexican restaurant to celebrate—Megan, Bree, Jax, and me. It being a free meal with margaritas and chips and guacamole and all the rest, naturally we said *yes*.

After a couple of drinks, Rob was a completely different guy than he'd been in the police station that night. We were joking and laughing and getting along great. Which, of course, made it easy for Megan to lob the question we were all dying to ask: "What happened with Colin? Did he get arrested?"

Rob was pretty jolly by that point and let out a hearty

laugh. "Nope. Nothing happened. He denied everything, just like Officer Wickham predicted. So what could they arrest him for? Since no one had filed a complaint about missing items, and there wasn't a report of theft, and the guy didn't have possession of any goods—stolen or otherwise—he walked." Rob scooped up some salsa with a tortilla chip, popped it in his mouth, and chewed loudly.

"They let him go?" Bree asked.

"Had to. They had nothing to charge him with."

"But what about the river?" I said around a bite of enchilada. "How'd he end up in the river?"

Rob shrugged. "Said he fell. No one believes him, but whatcha gonna do? My guess is, the person he was expecting to sell all that jewelry to—"

"The person he was supposed to meet instead of me—"

"Yeah, that person. Who knows? Maybe they gave him money up front, a down payment, and were pissed off because they were out the money and never got the jewelry—" Rob waved his arms like a conductor and we all shouted: "Because he left his briefcase in Sullivan's!"

Rob laughed. "The guy's an idiot."

"So they threw him in the river?" Bree asked, shocked.

"Probably a warning. *Don't do it again.* At least they didn't kill him."

I pictured getting thrown off the bridge just because someone wanted to make a point, falling into that cold, dark water with creatures lurking beneath the surface. Jax reached under the table to twine his fingers with mine. His hand was warm and strong and solid and safe. I let out a small contented sigh.

Rob washed a mouthful of burrito down with a swallow of margarita. "So, how's your Continental Breakfast Club coming along?" he asked. "Meet any new guys?"

"We haven't gone again yet," Bree said. "But we're going to—it's only been a week."

"We needed time to recuperate from our first meeting." Megan said. "I'm not in the market for a man anyway."

"Me neither." I grinned at Jax. "Bree is the only member currently manhunting."

Rob nodded. "I'm single you know."

Bree looked scandalized. Rob was easily twenty years older. "Oh, well...you're a great guy, but—" she stammered.

"Not for you," Rob said, slightly affronted. "All due respects, you're a bit young. Just wondering...were there single women at continental breakfast? You know, *closer to my age?*"

Rob Cramer wanted to join the Continental Breakfast Club? I threw a sideways glance at Megan and she gave a shrug. "As a matter of fact, there were several women there," I said.

"Not as many women as men," Bree added, "but they were there."

"So whadya think?" he asked. "Should I try it? Think I can join you sometime?"

Apparently, we were now the very best of friends. "Well...sure," I said.

"After we come back." Megan waved her fork. "The three of us are going on vacation in a few weeks, to the Outer Banks."

"Doing continental breakfast where the sea meets the sky," Bree said gleefully. "Breakfast at the inn where we're staying is ranked one of the best on the island."

"So is it the food you're going for—or the guys?" Rob asked.

I started to laugh and almost choked on a piece of enchilada. We'd made reservations for this trip long before forming the Continental Breakfast Club. Back then, the draw had definitely been the quality of the breakfast—not the men at the table.

"Guys like to eat. Good food draws men," Bree pointed out.

"Tell you what." Rob stabbed another piece of his giant burrito with his fork. "Once you're back, let me know when you're ready to have an old guy tag along."

"Okay, you're on," I said. Then we started to talk about Cape Hatteras and the North Carolina shore and Megan reminded us that we'd be there during hurricane season. So we reminded her that it was also prime vacation season and then shushed her by refilling her margarita glass and raising a toast to the Continental Breakfast Club, the best manhunting idea we'd ever had.

If you enjoyed this book ... I would be forever grateful if you would post a review on the site where you bought it.

The second book in *The Continental Breakfast Club* series, **Fresh Brewed**, is Bree's story. Please enjoy the following excerpt.

~

I was just one hour and eight minutes away from meeting the man of my dreams.

Okay, fine. Technically I was one hour and eight minutes of flying, plus two hours of driving, plus the rest of our three-hour layover in Atlanta away from meeting the man of my dreams.

No, he wasn't expecting me.

No, he didn't know I existed.

No, the phrase *man of my dreams* did not describe someone already on my radar. It was simply an all-encompassing description of the man I intended to meet while on vacation that week.

Please, let's not quibble.

The point is, as soon as our layover ended, we were going to fly to Norfolk where Megan, Allie, and I would pick up our rental car and drive to Hatteras Island for nine sun-drenched days at a charming beachfront inn, Sunrise Shores.

Anticipation rippled through me and I flipped open my guidebook to read a little more about our destination: *Hatteras Island is one of a string of barrier islands that make up the Outer Banks along the North Carolina coast. Miles of unspoiled white sand beaches, crystal blue water, and a temperate year-round climate make the islands a favorite for vacation getaways and destination weddings.*

It sounded like the perfect environment for romance. Sun, sand, sea...to say nothing of shirtless men in swim trunks, shimmering sunscreened skin, summery drinks with swizzle sticks, and—

What was that? Something had come over the public address system. I twisted toward Allie and Megan. "What did that announcement just say?"

"Shush." Megan waved a hand at me as she tilted her head to better hear.

"Ladies and gentlemen," an announcer said over the public address system, this time louder than before. "We apologize for the inconvenience, but Tropical Storm Drake has taken an unexpected turn toward the coast and has been upgraded to a hurricane. Mandatory evacuations have been ordered for the Outer Banks. For your safety, all flights to Norfolk have been cancelled at this time. We will be offering hotel accommodations to all affected passengers, and rescheduling flights once any danger is past. Thank you for your understanding. Again, we apologize and hope to have you on your way as soon as possible."

Stunned silence settled over the concourse and I looked around, desperately hoping to hear raucous laughter and, "Just kidding!" come blasting over the public address system next. I squeezed the guidebook between both hands, vaguely remembering the section about weather that described the Outer Banks as the highest risk area for tropical storms and hurricanes on the eastern seaboard.

We'd known there was a risk—had heard that Tropical Storm Drake was brewing in the Caribbean and moving north. But when all the experts confidently asserted Drake would pose no threat to land, that it would probably spin out onto the Atlantic where it would dissipate, we hadn't even given it a second thought.

So much for experts.

I'd been dreaming about this vacation since we booked it six months ago, how I would dash across the white sand beach the moment we arrived, skip through the surf, and twirl in the sun. Sunrise Shores, where we were staying, was renowned for its delectable continental breakfast and so, yes, I'd also let my daydreams slip into fantasies about meeting a fabulous man over omelets and fresh brewed coffee one morning, and how we'd spend a glorious week together. But now—

"Bree?"

I looked at Allie.

"Are you going to cry?"

"No, of course not." I blinked back the tears stinging my eyes. "It's just—I just want to be there, on the island. I really need this vacation." I could have gone into some protracted explanation about how teaching high school math leaves me burned out by the end of the school year, but we both knew it was more than that, so why bother?

The truth is, my boyfriend dumped me two months ago and it's been rough. So I just wanted to meet someone. Even if it ended up being nothing more than a shipboard romance—or, more appropriately, a beachside fling—that was okay. You know what they say: *the best way to get over one man is to get under another one.* Okay, fine, maybe I wouldn't take it that far, but it was vacation and I was determined to keep an open mind.

"Let's see what's going on." Megan swiped her phone and tapped the screen a couple of times to bring up a weather map showing swirling swaths of green, red, orange, and yellow out on the ocean heading straight for North Carolina. "Wow, if this actually hits land, we could be stuck here for—"

"God knows what will happen to Hatteras Island," Allie said.

That's when I really wanted to cry.

"We'd better get in line or we'll be sleeping in the airport." Megan slung her purse over her shoulder and headed toward the long line of people stretching out from the check-in counter.

A couple of hours later we were on a shuttle, packed shoulder-to-shoulder with other grounded passengers, all of us headed to a nearby Holiday Inn, restaurant coupons in hand. The airline employee had been very sympathetic. "We're so sorry. As soon as we get the *all clear*," she'd said, "we'll contact you by text and email with new flight arrangements and get you on your way as soon as possible. Meanwhile, enjoy dinner on us."

Nothing like dinner in some over-air-conditioned fast food joint in Atlanta when you were expecting to be bathed in balmy sea breezes while feasting on fresh lobster in a café overlooking the ocean.

"At least we get continental breakfast in the morning," Allie said as though she'd completely forgotten Sunrise Shores offered not just continental breakfast, but *gourmet* continental breakfast. "Never know who you'll meet."

Oh right. Like I was really going to meet someone at a continental breakfast at an airport hotel packed with people stranded in Atlanta who would all rather be somewhere else. *Come on.*

Allie had just gotten off the phone with her new boyfriend, Jax, who she'd met using our latest manhunting technique: dress professionally like you're on a business trip, then sneak into continental breakfast at an upscale hotel on a weekday morning.

Megan came up with the idea and it's almost brilliant. Think about it—crowded breakfast rooms provide the perfect excuse to share a table with someone you don't know. More specifically, with a successful man who could very well end up being *the one.* And it's easy to spot single guys in the morning—even though some men don't wear their wedding rings at hotel bars in the evening, it's a given that they all have them on at breakfast.

We knew right away there were some potential negatives to the idea. *Of course we did.* The guys are typically only going to be in town for a few days, so if one of us meets the ideal man, it could end up being a long-distance relationship. And it goes without saying that, at some point, one of us may have to 'fess up about why we really were at continental breakfast in the first place. But those negatives pale against the possibility of meeting *the one;* they're bridges to cross when and if they ever appear. Speed bumps on the road to love.

Technically, Allie didn't meet Jax at continental breakfast, anyway—she met him *because of* continental breakfast. But we still consider it a win for The Continental Breakfast Club because, without continental breakfast, she would never have met him at all. Which helps explain why I was entertaining such high hopes of meeting a guy this week at breakfast on the ocean.

As things stood, however, unless Drake blew itself out soon, my dreams were moot.

Anyway, so there we were in Atlanta, far enough inland to be safe from Drake's tantrum along the coast, spending our day in relative mundanity and bitching at Megan for taking calls from work when she was supposed to be on vacation. We hit the nearby mall for hours, then used our airline coupons for complementary dinner at a local restaurant across the street from our hotel. Finally, we picked up a bottle of red wine and a bag of chocolate-covered peanuts, and sprawled across the beds in our room to watch the classic romantic comedy, *You've Got Mail* on HBO.

When it was over and the credits had begun to roll, I let out a sigh. "I wish I could meet someone like Joe Fox," I said about the central character in the film. "He's perfect."

"It's easy to be perfect when someone else writes all of your lines," Megan pointed out.

"Don't be a buzz kill." I rolled onto my back on the bed. "Joe, Joe, wherefore art thou?"

Megan snorted. "Just like that, you're done with Mr. Darcy?"

"I forgot about him..." I fanned myself like I was over-heated. "Oh, Mr. Darcy, my feelings will not be repressed..."

"Or Jack Dawson?"

"You always liked him way more than I did." I looked at Allie. "Don't you think Joe Fox is the perfect guy?"

She smiled a little mysteriously.

"Forget her, she's too wrapped up in the real thing with Jax." Megan pointed the controller at the TV and clicked to the weather channel. "Let's see how many days we'll be vacationing near the lovely Atlanta airport," she said.

As soon as I saw the weatherman on the screen pointing at a swirling mass of blue, green, red, and yellow in the ocean off the eastern seaboard, and droning on about wind speed and storm surges, I said, "Shut it off, it's too depressing."

After another minute, Megan complied. "Let's go to sleep," she said. "Maybe things will change by morning."

"Tomorrow *is* another day." Allie added.

I threw a pillow at her.

The next morning dawned with clear skies, temperatures in the seventies, and text messages from our airline saying that flights were resuming immediately.

"Could this even be possible?" Allie asked.

"I guess tomorrow really is another day." I pulled open the curtains and blinked several times to adjust my eyes to the brilliant sun.

"Their email was probably hacked." Megan flipped on the television to check out the weather. "And someone's having a little fun sending out misleading emails."

"...just scraped the coast," a voice was saying over video footage taken during the night that showed heavy rain, trees bending, and waves surging up over sandy beaches and racing toward darkened homes. "Drake held the eastern seaboard at arm's length most of the night, steadily maintaining a distance about seventy miles out. In the wee hours, it surprised us all by veering to the northeast and out onto the ocean where it dissipated, putting an end to fears for the Outer Banks."

The station cut to a female reporter standing on the beach, impressive white-capped swells smashing onto the shore behind her. The camera panned over them as she spoke. "As the wind built last night and the sea rose, some buildings close to the beach sustained water damage from the action of the waves. There were even a few cases of damage from sudden wind shears," she said. "And, as you would expect, some areas experienced a bit of beach erosion. But Highway twelve survived intact—no wash-outs—and, overall, damage is extremely limited. We should all feel lucky, especially when you think of what might have been if Drake hadn't turned the other way. I'm happy to report that, most of the Outer Banks is no worse for the wear."

She went on to predict good weather for the next few days, but we quit listening because Allie had begun to dance around the room. "Breanna Mitchell, what are *you* going to do next?" she asked in an enthusiastic newscaster voice.

"I'm going to...the Outer Banks!" I began to dance with her. "Come on, Megan!"

Megan rolled her eyes. "I'm withholding my excitement until we actually have a flight. Thousands of people who got grounded have to, somehow, be shoehorned onto already scheduled flights—or extra planes have to be added. It's going to be a logistical nightmare." She pulled out her phone, dialed the airline, and was promptly put into a queue.

"Bzzzz. Buzz kill." Allie wagged a finger at her.

"I'm just being realistic."

"Debbie Downer, crabby apple, what are we to do with you?" Allie sang to Twinkle, Twinkle Little Star and started to dance again.

"Gorgeous men out on the beach, all of them within our reach…" I sang next.

Then we both rolled into the last line at the tops of our lungs, "Debbie Downer, crabby apple, what are we to do with you?"

Megan waved us quiet with a frantic hand and we both promptly shut up as she began talking to a booking agent. Minutes later, she had us scheduled on a flight for later that afternoon.

"Woohoo!" Allie crowed as we headed down to the hotel's continental breakfast. "We are almost out of here!"

Megan gave me a nudge. "Maybe Allie's right about today's continental breakfast. Maybe you'll meet your dream man this morning and this layover will be the best thing that ever happened."

I laughed giddily. "Nice thought but, actually, I'd rather meet him at the ocean. *Shirtless.*"

We rounded the corner into the breakfast room and simultaneously drew to an abrupt halt. People were *everywhere*. The place was packed.

"Omigod," Megan said.

The sound level was a dull roar. I looked across the room. Harried businessmen drinking coffee were trying to go over documents, a couple that looked suspiciously like newlyweds were huddled at a table in the corner, parents were trying to steer their families through the food choices, some little girl with adorable blond curls was screaming, "I want a waffle," at the same time some other kid was whining, "I was first," at the same time that four hyper children with powdered-sugared lips were swarming the donuts like addicts in search of their next fix, and an older boy was stiff-arming them, while repeating over and over, "No cuts. No cuts."

"They better not take all the custard-filled," Allie muttered.

"I'm sure the hotel has more." The expression on Megan's face belied the optimism of her words. "By the way, forget that I said anything about meeting my dream man this morning."

It looked like every passenger from every delayed flight had been put up at this Holiday Inn and then descended on breakfast at the same time. They probably all received the same text message we did and wanted to make sure the kids had a full stomach before heading to the airport.

I could hardly blame them. When I'm stuck somewhere and starving, my temperament isn't exactly a skip along the seashore. Kids are the same way, only worse—like to the one-thousandth power worse.

"Don't look now, but see that table with the three kids?" Megan asked under her breath and slightly tilted her head to the left.

I turned slowly to look across the room and spotted a family that had been seated a few rows ahead of us on the plane yesterday. The mother was trying to wipe off a toddler in a booster chair who was melting down, pulling at her hair with maple syrup-covered hands. "The ones that were on our plane?"

"They were?" Megan followed my gaze to make sure we were talking about the same people.

"Yeah, I recognize the dad," I said.

"Okay, well, I predict they'll be out of here in two minutes."

I watched the family like a rubbernecker gawking at an accident. As the mom struggled with the little girl, two slightly-older brothers were sucking chocolate milk into straws and spewing it at each other while ignoring their father who was demanding that they behave themselves... or else.

If those were my kids, I would be leaving in two minutes too. *Without them.* The family was like a funnel cloud onto itself.

"We'll have to hose off that table and chairs before we can use them." I looked around for the staff, and spotted two beleaguered high school kids who were having a hard enough time keeping the food trays filled, never mind cleaning up disastrous tables.

Megan inched toward the table, reaching it just as the father grabbed each of the boys by an arm and began to pull them toward the entranceway, while Mom scooped up the baby and followed them out. Megan was at the table before anyone else even realized a changeover was occurring.

She grinned at Allie and me. "Get some wet paper towel."

No kidding.

Once we had wiped everything down, we got toast, cereal, juice, and coffee and settled in to watch the show from our relatively safe spot in the corner. After a few minutes, Allie went to ask the staff if they had any custard-filled donuts.

"I don't know how parents travel with kids." Megan bit into her blueberry muffin. "There's no downtime. No relaxing cup of coffee. Every time you're about to catch your breath—"

A little boy at the next table spilled his half-pint carton of milk and then, after a heartbeat of dismay, gleefully slapped his hands into the puddle spreading across the table while his parents frantically tried to minimize the fallout.

Allie slid back into her chair. "The only donuts left are jelly-filled powdered sugar."

"Ergo, the kids with sticky faces." Megan nodded at another table, and we all watched, awestruck, as two boys with powdered sugar-covered mouths licked red jelly off their hands while their brother bent to lick the table.

"Maybe it's boys." As an only child, I had no idea if that was true, I just couldn't remember ever wanting sugar bad enough to lick tables to get it.

"Excuse me, do you need this chair?"

We all turned toward a woman about our age standing

near the empty chair at our table, a tray of food in her hands.

"No, go ahead. There's just three of us," Allie said.

Setting one hand on the back of the chair, she glanced around the room as if trying to figure out where to take it since there weren't any empty tables. I recognized her expression immediately, had seen it a million times before at the high school. It's the *I got Lunch A, and all my friends got Lunch B* face. That left-out feeling when there's no table where you belong, that outsider status that sends some kids into a restroom stall to eat their lunch in isolated mortification. The thought made my heart hurt.

"You want to join us?" I asked. "We have plenty of room."

A grateful smile lightened her face. The tension eased out of her as she set down her tray and slid into the empty chair. "Thanks. It's kind of wild in here."

"Beyond wild," Megan said.

"Imagine what it must be like at the airport." Allie spread some jam on her English muffin. "Probably total chaos. I'm Allie, by the way. This is Bree and Megan."

"Kristin. Kristin Caruso," our new tablemate said. "On the news they said people were sleeping all over the airport."

"That seals it for me," I said around a mouthful of fruity crunch cereal. "I vote we head to the airport as soon as we're done eating."

"Yeah." Megan nodded. "No doubt flights will be overbooked. Let's not risk getting bumped." Her phone vibrated on the table and she frowned at it. "Work. Again." She swiped the screen to read the message, then began to type in a response.

"You need to tell them you can't get a signal. Hurricane Drake and all that," Allie said. "It's the perfect excuse."

"Kind of a lie." I took another bite of cereal. "Since the signals are going to satellites and a storm down here won't affect those at all."

Allie rolled her eyes. "We both know what she really needs to do is tell work to bug off. But you know as well as I do that she won't. A little white lie accomplishes the same thing and that way she can actually have a vacation."

"Stop talking about me like I'm not here."

Kristin looked from one to the other of us. "I take it you've known each other for a long time."

"Obviously too long," Megan said dryly.

As Allie sputtered in mock indignation, I watched three college-age guys stumble into the breakfast room looking a little haggard, like their party from last night had just ended. "Check out these three. They were on our plane, too. Five rows up from the bathrooms, across the aisle."

"Rough night," Allie said.

"I bet they put everyone from our plane in this hotel." I perused the breakfast room. "Yeah, see the guy in the navy blue sweatshirt over there? He was in first class reading Time magazine."

"You remember random people from your plane?" Kristin asked. "I don't notice anyone unless they're weird, or make a scene, or something."

Allie snorted a laugh. "Guys. She remembers guys."

"Single ones," Megan added.

I shrugged sheepishly. "Hard to meet a good man these days."

"You don't happen to know any, do you?" Megan asked. "Because we would be grateful for the rest of our lives if you could introduce her to someone and put us out of this misery."

Kristin wrapped both hands around her coffee cup and smiled. "Well...I do happen to have brothers."

I set down my spoon. She seemed like a smart, attractive woman which boded well for siblings. "How many?"

"Two. Adam and Ethan."

"Single? In our general age group?" Allie asked before I could.

Kristin nodded.

"Well, then." I dusted my hands against each other playfully. "What are we waiting for?"

FRESH BREWED, excerpt by Pamela Ford ©2016

To receive news about upcoming books, giveaways, and special offers join Pamela Ford's mailing list at pamelaford.net.

ABOUT THE AUTHOR

PAMELA FORD is the award-winning author of contemporary and historical romance. She grew up watching old movies, blissfully sighing over the romance; and reading sci-fi and adventure novels, vicariously living the action. The combination probably explains why the books she writes are romantic, happily-ever-afters with plenty of plot —and often, lots of laughter.

After graduating from college with a degree in Advertising, Pam spent many years as a copywriter and freelance writer before inserting a plot twist in her career path and writing her first book.

Pam has won numerous awards including the Booksellers Best, the Laurel Wreath, and a gold medal IPPY in the Independent Book Publisher Awards. She is a National Readers' Choice Awards finalist, a Maggie Awards finalist, a Kindle Book Awards finalist, and a two-time Golden Heart Finalist. More than a half million copies of her books have been sold worldwide.

Sign up for Pam's mailing list at: www.pamelaford.net
Contact: pamelafordbooks@gmail.com
Visit: facebook.com/pamelafordbooks

Made in the USA
Columbia, SC
22 July 2020